A Thread of Secrets

Tatiana Tierney

A Thread of Secrets

Paperback ISBN 978-1-3999-6491-3
Hardback ISBN 978-1-7384090-2-0
E-Book ISBN 978- 1-7384090-0-6

First published as a debut novel in Ireland by Tatiana Tierney in 2024
Printed in the European Union
www.tatianatierney.com

My endless gratitude to my husband, Niall
for his support, time and encouragement.

Prologue

Awake, May 1969

From where she sat on the wooden bench under a hawthorn tree, Grace tried to gather her restless thoughts, observing her garden. A gentle breeze caressed her dark, slightly grey hair. She was forty-seven years old but thought the many wrinkles on her face and her pale complexion made her look older. A dreadful nightmare had awoken her early, so she just sat there for a while, watching the birds eating from the birdfeeders until she felt her heart rate return to normal. Presently, she found herself able to think about the nightmare, to recall it moment by moment.

She was back in India, where she had lived in the 1940s. It was the day Grace gave birth to her child at the house she had been brought to by force. Her beloved maid, Zia, was in the house and was standing next to her. There was dead silence in the room. Grace lay motionless in bed, breathing weakly. In Zia's arms there was a newly born child, who wasn't making a sound. A small bird flew in through the open window. The bird's beak opened, but it didn't make a sound either. Grace bit her lips and was still clutching the white sheets, which were drenched in blood. Then she noticed that Zia was trembling in fear. As Grace stared at her, everything became blurred. She could barely make her out as Zia began to hide the baby in what looked like a large, thick blanket, whispering something in her own Hindu language.

Then Grace was outside, beneath a glowing red sky. She was wearing a white robe, her hair loose, and in her arms was the baby, her baby. Red flames enveloped her from head to toe. Though she wanted more than anything to look at her child, her body didn't obey her wish. And when eventually she did look, all she saw were her empty hands. The child was gone. She emitted a scream, which echoed into the void. The nightmare ended.

Grace's throat still ached from the scream long after she had woken up. A fire was burning in her chest. Her soul hadn't found peace. The tears came, streaming down her face. Sitting up in bed, she had looked down at her hands as though they might contain an answer as to why the awful nightmare had affected her so badly this time. It had often come, haunting her with its painful unanswered questions, but there was something different this time. *What* was it?

The baby. For the first time, the baby had not lain still in Zia's arms. It had *moved.* With that realisation came the question. Might it be possible that on that terrible night so many years ago, her child hadn't died after all?

Part I

England 1934–1943

The birth of Grace

A mother's story

The year was 1934. One morning, Grace was called by her grandmother, Elizabeth Bellmore, as she passed by her grandmother's study in their home, White Cliffs Manor.

"Grace, dear child, come in here. I want to have a word with you."

Grace stood at the doorway, trying to hide the photograph in her hand. Though she loved her grandmother dearly, she always felt slightly nervous in her company.

"Come, come," Elizabeth said briskly. "Sit down." She pointed to the dark green leather chair.

Grace sat, facing her nana – as she called her in private – across the vast oak desk. Her grandmother took off her glasses.

"You have asked me about your parents often enough." She paused for a second and then, with a rare trace of emotion in her voice, said, "I told you about my son, your father, George, remember?"

Grace nodded. She remembered every word.

Her father had been a kind and intelligent young man. He had become an officer in the British Army, serving in the First

World War. At the end of the war, he met Nora, her mother, in a hospital in France where she was working as a nurse. Unfortunately, he never fully recovered from the horrific injuries he suffered during the last year of the war, and he died a few years later, just before Grace was born in 1922. Upset by this recollection, Grace hunched her shoulders and looked down sadly.

Elizabeth continued. “You also know that your mother was from Donegal in Ireland.” When Elizabeth mentioned Ireland, her voice became more upset, but she quickly pulled herself together. “And they lived there after they came back from France.”

“Nana, my parents lived in Ireland? I didn’t know that. Why not here, with you?” Grace knew that her grandmother wouldn’t like the interruption but couldn’t resist asking.

Elizabeth took a deep breath before she replied. “They had their own reasons, my dear.” She looked down and fiddled with her glasses briefly.

Grace sensed there was something more, but her grandmother wasn’t prepared to tell her, something she felt even more sure of when Elizabeth changed the subject quickly.

“Your mother wanted me to tell you about her and her story. I think now that you are twelve years old, it is time for you to learn a little bit more about why you came to England to live here at White Cliffs Manor.”

Elizabeth explained that Grace's mother was in the last months of her pregnancy when her father died, and she was very weak.

"Nora and I started to write to each other," she said. "We were both lonely widows. I was over the moon when I learned about you coming into this world soon. Unfortunately, I was here in England, and your mother was in Ireland. The only way to stay connected was through your mother's letters. She told me how she spent most of her time sitting on a bench under a hawthorn tree in her garden, gazing at the ocean. She lived in a wild part of Ireland famous for its wide sandy beaches, surrounded by dunes and green fields dotted with sheep, and where the wind, sun and rain could all come in a single day. The stone walls next to the threebedroom house she had inherited led down to the beach and, beyond that, the restless Atlantic Ocean."

Elizabeth turned in her chair and looked out the window at the bluewhite stripe of sea in the distance. Grace noticed a slight dreaminess in her grandmother's eyes and was afraid to interrupt. Also, gazing out of the window, she could see the sea and the beach where she loved to spend time. Grace tried to imagine the Atlantic Ocean where her mother had walked on the white sandy beach with her.

"Nana, did Mummy tell you anything about me in her letters?" asked Grace softly. She lowered her tone because she didn't want to take away that rare shine in her grandmother's eyes. On the other hand, she wanted to hear more.

"She did," said Elizabeth, and went on to tell Grace the story of her birth using the words in her mother's letters:

> "One day, when the weather was warm and sunny, your mother was enjoying watching the white foamy waves crashing on top of each other and listening to the sound of seagulls. She turned her head up and noticed a beautiful branch of hawthorn above her. It was mid-May when hawthorn trees blossom and produce a light, sweet aroma. Your mother's legs were covered with a woolly throw, and her back rested against a soft cushion. She was comfortable and lost in time. She didn't pay much attention to the pain rising and falling inside her. After all, she was in the late stages of her pregnancy. Some discomfort was surely to be expected.
>
> "When she realised her waters were breaking and she was ready to give birth, it was almost too late. Your mother started to panic. She tried to stand up, but the pain had increased to the point that it pushed her back onto the bench. At the same time, it was difficult for her to sit on the hard surface. She tried to move into a more comfortable position with her hands behind her back, holding up her weight. Eventually, her legs gave way, and she slowly slid to the ground with her back to the bench. Thankfully, her neighbour and friend, who lived

next door, was outside in her garden at the time and heard your mother's scream.

"Nora! Have your waters broken?"

"Yes. I do not think I can make it to the house."

"Let me help you up. Try, Nora, try."

"I cannot do it!"

"All right, my dear, stay where you are. I will get everything we need from the house."

"The rest of what happened was a blur for your mother. She vaguely remembered that her neighbour helped to move her to the throw, which was placed on the ground. Then she heard her saying 'push, push' and herself crying out in pain. The next thing, you had safely entered this world. Your mother's abiding memory of that moment was looking up at the beautifully blossomed hawthorn branch above her when she heard your first cry. She took this as a sign of protection and thanked the hawthorn.

"Nora, congratulations. You have a beautiful, healthy baby girl. You are a very brave and strong woman. Well done!"

"I cannot thank you enough, my dearest friend." Nora was out of breath.

"What are you going to call your little angel?"

"Grace," Nora immediately replied, because she had

already decided on the name.

"What a beautiful name."

"My angel. My Grace."

"Your mother greeted you with a smile. The beauty of this moment was made more special by the warmth of the sun and the gentle touch of sea air. Your mother told me that she was overwhelmed with her emotions. She gazed lovingly into your wise green eyes and stroked your soft black hair."

After hearing this, tears started to fall from Grace's eyes.

Elizabeth immediately reacted. "No need to cry, my dear child."

She was never one for tears or strong displays of emotion. The lovely dreaminess in her eyes was gone.

"I'm sorry, Nana," said Grace, wiping away her tears.

"Were you not lucky to arrive so healthy and beautiful?"

Grace nodded. "The photograph?" She tentatively pulled it out from her pocket.

"That was taken about seven months later. And yes, the hawthorn tree in the photo of you and your mother is the same one you were born under."

"I always knew there was something special about it."

Elizabeth continued the story.

"It was less than a year after, that your mother died from tuberculosis. I had done everything I could think of to persuade Nora to move to White Cliffs, but to no avail. Nora wanted to be able to visit your father's grave and loved her home in Donegal too much. We finally agreed that I would help out later with your education. For the time being, Nora said, she just wanted to be with you, her daughter, in Ireland. I accepted that. One day, sad news arrived from Ireland that your mother had passed away. I, of course, went there straight away to bring you to White Cliffs, your new home. You were two years of age. It was the kind neighbour who suggested I bring a clipping from the hawthorn tree, putting it in some earth so that it would stay alive on the journey back here. I planted it in the big garden pot first, and then after a few years, as you will remember, we replanted it together in the garden."

That corner of the garden with the hawthorn tree would become Grace's favourite place, where she would spend a few minutes every day with the photograph in her hands. She couldn't explain it, but she had always felt a strong connection with her mother through that tree. She treasured those moments the most, and right then she looked lovingly out of the window towards the garden.

"You can go now, my dear. I am sure that you want to go to the garden. You need time to digest what I have just told you."

Grace knew when her grandmother also wanted to be left alone. She thanked her and decided not to ask more questions.

She was overwhelmed and her mind was in overdrive. She needed space, just like her grandmother noted, so she could imprint this new information into her memory forever.

Life in England

Childhood friend

Five years later, on a Saturday afternoon, Grace and her best friend, Molly Baker, were lolling about on Grace's bed, talking. Grace had met Molly in a private school when she was getting her secondary education. She was the only friend Grace had ever had. Grace knew that her grandmother had the kind of reputation in society that meant she would only socialise with the upper classes, as she considered herself much closer to the upper class due to her financial status. The Baker family was middle class, but it didn't bother Grace. If it weren't for the school they attended, she probably would never have met Molly. For some unknown reason, the two girls clicked from day one.

They went horse riding together, played the piano together, and read books aloud to each other. The only thing Grace did without Molly was drawing. Lately, Molly had started going to a local dancing club in the evenings, something Grace had no interest in, even if her grandmother *would* have allowed it, which she wouldn't. It was as if Molly were growing up more quickly than Grace, even though they were both now seventeen years of age.

Like many young girls at the end of the 1930s, they both followed the fashion trends set by actresses like Betty Grable, whom Molly idolised. Molly styled her hair short and curly like Betty's, while Grace preferred to keep her hair long and wavy like Ava Gardner and Vivien Leigh. Molly often complained about the colour of her eyes. They were the same colour as her hair, brown. She wanted to dye her hair blonde to stand out, but her mother wouldn't allow it. Regarding dress style, Molly's choice was the shorter, the better. Unlike her friend, who preferred floral patterns, Grace gravitated towards long dresses with pastel colours such as peach, sky blue or green. The girls had their differences and similarities. Usually, they joked about them. They had both started to pay more attention to their looks, and the time had arrived for them to share their likes or dislikes about boys too.

That Sunday, Grace was nervous because it was the first time Molly had come around in almost two months. Molly was upset and Grace had an idea why. She got straight to the point.

"You know," she said with a firm tone. "I never had any interest in that boy. I never did anything to make him think I had, either. Is that what you are upset about?"

The boy was someone Molly had met at the local dancing club and had fallen for, but when she had introduced him to

Grace, he had shifted his attention to her.

"What boy?" Molly pretended she didn't understand.

"You know, Molly. You introduced me to him a few months back."

"Ah, is that the one who was sending letters and flowers to you?" said Molly sulkily. "And invited you to a party last Saturday? I wasn't interested."

"I didn't go to that party and the same with the letters – never opened. You could have told me, you know, that it was bothering you."

"It wasn't really. Many fellows around."

"Then, why didn't you come to see me? Ah, I know, the flowers, right? I can tell you Nana enjoyed them very much. She was surprised to see the flowers in her study. I said it was from her admirer." Both girls saw the funny side of their misunderstanding and laughed.

Then Grace changed the subject.

"Well, forget about him. Stay for lunch, won't you?"

"I don't think your grandmother would be pleased."

Grace couldn't disagree. There was always a coolness in the way her grandmother greeted Molly.

"The only reason she lets you be friends with me is because my father sometimes buys horses for rich people from her."

"I wouldn't say that, Molly. Horses have nothing to do with our friendship."

"We are too poor for her liking. And I would say she is terrified that you will fall in love with my brother." Molly laughed, but it had a hard quality to it.

Grace realised Molly was hurt by Nana's behaviour. Over the past few years, she had found herself more and more at odds with her beloved grandmother, even if she rarely voiced it. Her nana wasn't the kind of person you argued with lightly. Elizabeth's way of giving her opinion in public was more careful; she would only make a bold remark on something if she knew the audience and felt confident. Grace and Molly were from a new generation, but Grace admired her grandmother for the strength of her opinions which weren't swayed by changing times.

"Nana means well," she said finally to Molly in defence. "She has her ways, but she has a good heart."

"Well, anyway" – Molly's voice this time was filled with sadness – "she doesn't need to worry, because we are moving to London next month. My parents are getting separated. So, I won't be coming around anymore."

Grace understood why Molly was so upset and hadn't visited for so long. It wasn't just about a silly boy. Her friend's life was about to change, and that change probably wouldn't be for the better. If Molly's parents separated, it would mean her father would be the decisionmaker, especially about their finances. Unfortunately, after separation or divorce, women were usually left with very little financial support. Grace had learned that at a very young age from her grandmother. Molly's mother was one of those unfortunate women. Molly told Grace that her father recently became bankrupt and therefore couldn't support his daughter's plan to attend Oxford University together with Grace.

Grace tried to say something supportive to Molly.

"Look, we are both upset that we won't go to university together. I will miss you dearly, but you and your mum will still be here in England. Oxford University is not the be all and end all; London has plenty of good universities."

"It's not up to me anymore. My mother can't tell me yet about her plans. I have no idea where we will live, what she will do and, most importantly, what I will do. No idea at all."

"It all will work out in the end. Don't worry. This unpleasant time for you and your mum will pass. I am sure she needs time to organise everything and will let you know about her plans soon. Just stay in touch with me please, will you?"

"Grace, you are my dearest friend! Of course, I want to stay in touch with you, but ..."

"Shh, it's fine." Grace, spotting tears in Molly's eyes, leaned over and gave her a cuddle.

There was an awkward moment when they both realised that it was probably their last meeting, and they had no idea when they would see each other again. Grace offered her friend a cup of tea and asked for a tray with tea and biscuits to be brought up to her room, where she knew Molly would feel more comfortable, rather than in the drawing room downstairs. They talked about the Bellmore family horses and, in particular, the one which Molly liked. Molly said that she would miss him. Grace promised her friend that she could always come back and ride him. It was hard for both of them to keep up the conversation. Grace didn't want Molly to leave, but she knew there was nothing she could do about it. When they finished tea, Molly got up and went to the bookshelf, picking up one of the books. It was *Pride and Prejudice*.

"Did you read this? Any good?"

"I just started, and, yes, I like it. If you like romance, it is a great read. Would you like to have it?"

"Thanks, but would you not like to finish it first?"

"Don't worry, I think we have another edition in Nana's study. So, please take it. I want you to have it. Please, Molly."

"All right then. It will be a memento of you. You know I am not a big reader, but I promise you that I will read this one." She said it with a broken smile. "Wait, but I don't have anything for you."

"Don't worry Molly. I am sure we will see each other before you leave, won't we?"

Molly nodded, looking out of the window. "Sure."

Elizabeth Bellmore

A loving grandmother

The year was 1943, and war still raged on. Grace was having lunch with her grandmother in the dining room of White Cliffs Manor. The manor had got its name because of its location near the white cliffs along the south-east coast of England, close to a small town called Seafield. Grace knew that the house and the estate, which Elizabeth Bellmore had inherited from her parents, was her grandmother's most prized possession. For three generations, the Bellmore family had been responsible for breeding the best horses in the country. The house was built in Edwardian style, in red brick with stained glass doors and white-framed windows. In front of the house stood two big statues of white horses made from local stone. There was a huge oak tree on the left side of the house and a driveway surrounded by tidy green shrubs. This haven was hidden from the public eye and gave its residents privacy and peace.

The dining room they ate in was bright and airy. Grace sat to the right of her grandmother, who was placed at the top of the long table. Grace recalled her grandmother had hired an expensive interior designer from London some years back to decorate the house. The fabric of the curtains and furniture matched and were in a combination of two colours, pale pink and dark purple, with a white pattern in between.

While Elizabeth recounted the day's events, Grace mused about how wonderful her grandmother was in spite of her sternness. There was a lot to admire about her. How she had held on to the house and the family business as a widow, even during the difficult years of the First World War and, in its aftermath, the Spanish flu, which took so many lives. How she took on the raising of Grace without complaint, making sure she received a good education. How she kept a diary for everything, and her inability to tolerate people who ran late for a meeting or dinner.

Even though Elizabeth wasn't beautiful in the common sense of the word, she had charisma. People were attracted to her. And though she didn't hold a title, many of her friends called her Lady Elizabeth. She always followed ladies' fashion and was known in many upmarket boutiques in London for her choice of clothing. The same standards were applied to Grace too. When she had been a little girl, she was always dressed like a princess – only the best fabric for clothing, only the best hats and handbags.

Everything Grace knew about social etiquette, she had

learned from her grandmother, who was always generous with compliments when they attended a dinner or party together away from home. Sometimes, Grace overheard her grandmother's friends saying how they envied her for having such a gorgeous and welleducated granddaughter. Elizabeth would proudly reply that Grace was a Bellmore.

On the other hand, at times, Grace knew that she annoyed her beloved nana when she displayed character traits which reminded her of Nora. However, Grace grew up obedient and grateful. She didn't want to upset her loving grandmother and therefore learned to keep her opinions to herself. They were just from two different generations.

"I have some good news," began her grandmother brightly.

"Did Molly come back?" asked Grace. She heard how foolish it sounded as soon as she asked it. After Grace had completed her degree at Oxford, she moved to London to volunteer with the Red Cross. She still hadn't made any new friends and had no idea which part of London the Baker family had moved to. Grace missed Molly.

Her grandmother frowned. "Molly? Who is Molly? Do you mean Molly Baker? Of course not."

"Oh. I suppose not."

"It is much more exciting than that."

Was Grace imagining it, or was her grandmother nervous? If so, it was a first.

"We have been invited to a rather grand dinner, by Lord Clifford, no less."

Lord Clifford was a wealthy industrialist from York and was a widower. Recently, Grace had learned a lot about him from her grandmother, who had known him for many years through a mutual interest in tea. Elizabeth loved tea. So did Grace. Lord Clifford's father had strong connections with the East India Company, the British-owned trading corporation that was the world's largest and most powerful, and had diversified from cotton into the tea business, which he had passed to his son. Grace heard that his family had acquired a huge estate in India from a maharajah and then developed it into a tea plantation. The tea he imported from India was of the highest quality and was distributed throughout the British Empire. Due to his enormous wealth, he ranked among the highest echelons of British society.

Only when Elizabeth began talking of Lord Clifford's two sons did Grace understand what was behind her grandmother's growing interest in him. The eldest, James, she said, was a disappointment. He was raised in boarding school before going on to finish his education in the military academy Sandhurst. He passed out with the rank of second lieutenant, assigned to the Royal Scots Fusiliers as his regiment. But despite this promising start, he had since gained a reputation for being illmannered and a drunkard. He was an inveterate philanderer and was still unmarried at thirty-nine. At that time, he was serving in India.

Lord Clifford's second son, Oliver, on the other hand, was a very impressive young man by all accounts. Handsome, too. He was well brought up, with excellent manners and a university education. As far as Elizabeth understood things, he was now the expected heir of the Cliffords' tea empire rather than his older brother.

"Nana, I don't see what any of this has to do with me," said Grace, warily.

"Heavens above," Elizabeth whispered to herself, barely managing to hide her irritation.

"You have grown into an appealing young lady, Grace. Educated and cultured too. We may not be of the upper class, but you are the daughter of a gentleman, which makes you a respectable choice for any man. And I will not be around forever."

"Nana, please don't say that."

"It will happen sooner or later, my dear. And you need to understand your value. I do not want you marrying someone unworthy of you."

Grace didn't have to ask. She knew her grandmother meant Molly's brother, who had always been an example of an unsuitable husband in her nana's eyes.

"We have to get ready for dinner at Lord Clifford's. You

must take it seriously, Grace," Elizabeth said sternly.

"But, Nana, I promised to do more work with the Red Cross."

"Nonsense. You have given them enough of your time. We will go to London together next week to see my seamstress to make you a new dress."

That was how Grace learned that her grandmother had all but arranged her marriage to a man she had never met, and it seemed there wasn't a thing she could do about it.

London 1943

Friends' reunion

During that week with her grandmother in London, Grace visited the hospital where she had volunteered and saw her old friend Molly Baker walking across the hall into one of the wards.

"Molly," she shouted. "It's me, Grace."

"Grace!" Molly was beaming as she walked towards Grace. The two friends embraced.

"Look at you!" Molly observed Grace quickly. "I missed you so much!" She took Grace's hand in hers as if she feared Grace would leave her.

"I missed you too, Molly." Grace put her other hand on top of Molly's to assure her that she wasn't going anywhere. "I'm sorry I lost touch with you. Why did you never write to me? I didn't know where you had gone. I waited for you to send me a message."

"What could I write, Grace?" An awkward few seconds silenced them both. "Let's have something to eat, and I will tell all," said Molly, who seemed in a rush to leave the hospital.

They went for lunch together in one of the pubs local to the hospital. While they were walking, Grace could not help but notice the scenes of destruction caused as a result of the intensive bombing of the city by the Luftwaffe. She was impressed by the stoicism of Londoners and how they patiently waited in queues to receive their daily food rations.

When Molly and Grace arrived at the pub, they sat down and were momentarily silent after witnessing the scenes of destruction around them. They ordered food and Molly started to fill Grace in on her life since she had moved to London. It was a sad story. After her parents had separated and her brother had been killed in action, her mother fell apart and started to drink heavily. Molly said that she saw her father again only once after the separation; it was at her brother's funeral. Last week she decided to volunteer at the hospital, but it was too hard for her, as the injured soldiers in pain reminded her of her brother. Now, due to financial pressures and her mother's vulnerable state, she desperately needed a job.

"Oh, Molly, I'm so sorry. I can only imagine how difficult it has been for you and your mother."

"No, Grace, you can't imagine. It's bloody hard! Too much, and all on my shoulders." Molly carefully, but quickly, recoiled from another attempt by Grace to embrace her. Her eyes were full of tears. When she spoke again, her voice was sharp.

"I need a job urgently. A job that pays. I have no one to support me financially."

"I see. Let me think. I might be able to help."

Grace told Molly about Lord Clifford and his business. She knew from her grandmother that Lord Clifford's sister, Louise, was looking for a French teacher for her two daughters.

"I know you spoke French very well. How is your French now?"

"I managed to keep it up … I could do this job!" Molly perked up.

"Jolly good. I will get Louise's phone number for you tomorrow," Grace promised.

They kept chatting for an hour. Grace also shared details about her life over the last few years, which had been mostly taken up with her studies.

"You mean no personal life?"

"My personal life? You know me," said Grace, smiling. Then, not to seem too boring, she told Molly more about Lord Clifford, about his vast estate, about the fact that he and her grandmother seemed hellbent on setting her up with Lord Clifford's youngest son, Oliver. She told Molly about the upcoming dinner party.

"Wow. How do you feel about that?" asked Molly.

How did she feel about it? At first, Grace had felt frightened and angry. But as the days passed since lunch with her grandmother, Grace had found herself daydreaming about this mysterious Oliver. It was so much more pleasant to imagine she might fall in love with him, that he might be kind and caring.

"A wedding soon! I can see you already in your most beautiful white dress. And all your admirers along the street watching you with open mouths," joked Molly.

"Don't get carried away. I haven't met him yet. With your imagination you could write a book."

"Still," said Molly with a cheeky smile, "it's exciting."

"Molly, don't tease me." Grace felt her face flush. She looked away, flustered.

"Hmm, I hope this time you will accept the flowers."

They both laughed, remembering that poor boy who had sent Grace flowers and love letters she didn't even open.

"Lucky you, Grace. You attract attention like a magnet. If I were you, I wouldn't think twice when such an opportunity arises."

"Molly, you are beautiful and smart. In due time, you will meet your prince. You shouldn't worry about it too much."

"So many of our princes have been killed." Molly suddenly started to cry.

Grace, remembering that her friend recently lost her brother, hugged her and cried too.

"Molly, I will do everything to help you. Give me a couple of days. What is your address now? How will I find you?"

"Take this. There is a phone number at the end." Molly took

a piece of paper from her pocket. "I always keep a note with my address on it, just in case."

Grace read the address. "Oh, it's so far from here and I heard rather grim comments about that area of London."

"Yes, I know. It's not the best place, but it's what we got from my father. His generous gift. But let's not go there. He doesn't exist for me anymore. You don't need to worry about me, Grace. I just need a job and all will be sorted."

"All right, Molly. I will be in touch with you soon. In the meantime, please look after yourself," said Grace once they got outside.

"Why? Do I look so bad?" Molly put her hand into her little handbag to find a mirror.

"That's not what I meant. You just look a bit tired, and you need a good sleep. That's all. Please take care of yourself. Promise?"

"I promise. Thanks, Grace. It's so difficult to let you go. Wouldn't it be nice if we lived near each other again? I miss our time together, our Saturdays. Do you remember how we dreamed that we would marry two brothers, end up in the same family, and never be separated?"

"I do, Molly. We were young and full of childish fantasies. I guess it happens sometimes. Let's believe in miracles. I also want us to live much closer to each other, to have an opportunity to spend more time together. Who knows, it might happen. Dreams do come true, sometimes."

"I wish they would hurry up," said Molly, more to herself than to Grace, as she was already walking away.

Dinner at Lord Clifford's

An unexpected guest

All the guests were seated in the drawing room of Lord Clifford's mansion in York, which comprised a high ceiling, tall windows and furniture decorated in an expensive fabric. The focal point in the room was a Georgian-style fireplace. It was made from white marble with sleek lines and intricate carving – the epitome of the rich and classic beauty of that era.

Grace warmed quickly to Lord Clifford when she met him. He was around sixty years old, like her grandmother, and standing next to one another, he and Elizabeth seemed well-matched. Elizabeth, a statuesque woman with aquiline features, wore a light grey tweed skirt with a matching cardigan over a navyblue blouse, while Lord Clifford sported a white shirt with a blue cravat around his neck. Both had pale grey hair.

When Lord Clifford explained that the dinner was only for family members, Grace noticed her grandmother had a look of satisfaction on her face. Grace felt slightly nervous and uncomfortable in her new dress made from green satin that matched her emerald eyes. Her grandmother and Lord Clifford kept glancing towards the window. It was almost comical how impatient they were for the two brothers to arrive. Louise, her husband, Fred, and their two daughters sat comfortably by the fireplace. The gentle crackling of the fire seemed to have a relaxing effect on Louise and her family. Fred was a big man in his mid-fifties. He sat quietly with his eyes half closed, probably dozing. He was the only one not interested in what was going on around him. A burly butler with a surly expression on his face stood motionless at the front door ready to open it at any time.

Grace moved away from her grandmother when the maid brought glasses of champagne for everybody. She could still hear the conversation between Elizabeth and Lord Clifford. He was explaining that he'd tasked Oliver with finding his brother in London and bringing him home for dinner. Lord Clifford wasn't eager to see his eldest son, but he wanted James to be there when Oliver was introduced to Grace. Then he told Elizabeth about the tradition in their family of the eldest son always being married before the youngest, but that this time, Lord Clifford would be the one deciding which of them would be first.

"For now, James is always the *first* to empty my bank account. I cannot wait for when Oliver has a family and I will be able to pass my estate and business to him." Elizabeth nodded in support of his hopes and desire.

"Here they are!" exclaimed Lord Clifford, as a car drove up the driveway. They all went to the window. Grace felt a flutter in her stomach as the driver's door opened and a tall, blondhaired man got out. But instead of walking to the house, he went around to the passenger door and opened it.

"There is someone with him," whispered Elizabeth.

They all watched as a young woman got out and smiled at him. Then she looked towards the house.

"Molly," said Grace, in amazement. "It's Molly!"

The silence that followed continued until the butler opened the door and announced their arrival. Oliver and Molly entered the room. Now, even Grace found she couldn't speak. It was Lord Clifford's sister, who was apparently unaware of her brother's plan to introduce Oliver to Grace, who broke the silence by welcoming her nephew and Molly.

"Everybody, please meet Molly …" Oliver hesitated.

"Molly?" Lord Clifford interrupted and looked at Molly as if she were a ghost.

Elizabeth stood in shock, and Grace, reading her grandmother's expression, could tell that she was unable to utter a word. Lord Clifford introduced himself to Molly and then quickly moved away from the unexpected guest to introduce Elizabeth and Grace to Oliver. Molly's smirk at them didn't help at all.

"I do not understand," Elizabeth whispered to Grace, her eyes widened in surprise.

Neither did Grace. Yes, she had helped Molly by getting her a job, but this was a remarkable transformation for Molly, who had gone from being a needy girl a month ago to now going out with a wealthy bachelor. *No, it can't be like that*, thought Grace.

"How do you know each other?" Elizabeth asked Oliver, while trying to keep her head up and pretending that it was just a polite question, nothing more. Grace noticed that her grandmother seemed suddenly greyer and older.

"We have got to know each other lately, Mrs Bellmore," replied Oliver. "Since Grace secured Molly a position in my aunt's house." He nodded at Grace and thanked her for that. Then Oliver told everybody how he liked to visit his aunt's house because he loved her homemade pies, especially her apple pie.

When Oliver turned to Louise, begging her for the recipe, Elizabeth said to Grace. "It is obvious that his interest was not *only* in his aunt's baking skills."

Grace couldn't bring herself to return her grandmother's angry stare. She kept saying to herself that Oliver had simply invited Molly to dinner out of courtesy, as someone who worked for his aunt's family. She caught herself examining Oliver. He was a tall, handsome man with thick blond hair and was dressed smartly. His glasses meant Grace couldn't properly see the colour of his eyes but she thought they were greyish. From the way he kept briefly touching his glasses like he wanted to take them off, she could tell that they irritated him. She knew from her grandmother that Oliver's poor eyesight was the reason he wasn't at the front line. Despite the glasses being too big, Grace could see the resemblance to his father. She glanced over to Molly who was wearing a dark blue knee-length dress. It wasn't Molly's favourite colour, but it sat nicely on her figure. And she had her hair done.

"Molly, I'm so glad to see you." Grace quickly walked over to her friend, hugged and kissed her on the cheek and briefly said hello to Oliver. Then took her by the arm and led her away before Elizabeth said anything more.

"Where is James?" Grace heard Lord Clifford's nervous voice as they moved off.

"How did you get on with the girls?" Grace asked Molly quietly and they both looked at Louise's daughters who were still sitting by the fire. Grace wondered if Molly's attention was actually on teaching the girls French or on something else. She felt a bit lost about what to think of her friend at that moment.

For a few minutes the hum of conversation filled the room. While Molly told Grace about her new job, Grace could overhear the heated discussion between Oliver and his father not far away from them. Oliver fiddled nervously with his glasses.

"Father, please hear me out," he said, so loudly that everybody could hear.

Grace instantly glanced at the butler who patiently waited for the right moment, who then quietly approached Lord Clifford to inform him that dinner was ready. Lord Clifford nodded his thanks and moved away from his son, mumbling that they would continue this conversation later. He invited everyone to the dining room. Oliver returned to escort Molly there as this was her first time in the house.

While they walked towards the dining room, Lord Clifford approached Elizabeth and whispered in her ear, "There is nothing to worry about. I will talk to him later."

Elizabeth, in response, whispered back, "I know this girl and am very surprised at Oliver's behaviour, but I believe it is just an impulsive decision."

Lord Clifford shrugged and rolled his eyes. They were talking to each other as if Grace wasn't present. Grace then noticed a brief touch of hands between Oliver and Molly. Her doubts crashed. It was obvious that the two of them were much closer than she thought.

Dinner conversation covered various topics, with everyone speaking at some point. There were also a few awkward silences when Molly said something silly or laughed too loudly. Grace and her grandmother were sitting opposite Oliver and Molly, so it was easy to watch the two of them together. Although

Grace didn't know much about Oliver, she knew Molly very well, and her happy feeling at meeting her dear friend after many years apart was fading away quickly.

Elizabeth looked over the table to Molly and said in a stern voice under her breath, "I would not lose the run of yourself."

"Nana!"

"I always thought that girl was a bit over the top."

"She is fine, Nana. She actually speaks French fluently, you know. That's why she could get that job. She can now provide for herself and her mother." Surprising herself, Grace defended Molly.

"French! Quelle surprise," quipped Elizabeth.

"Nana … she could hear you."

"I am getting too old, my dear, and do not have time for such frivolous girls."

Grace was shocked and surprised that her grandmother could be so caustic. She decided it was best not to reply. Elizabeth looked tired. Her grey hair was almost white. Grace wondered if her grandmother was being honest about her health. She had noticed that the doctor's visits to their house had increased lately. Grace made a promise to herself that she would talk to her grandmother upon their return to White Cliffs.

The main dish arrived – beef wellington with roasted vegetables and potatoes – and distracted Elizabeth as it was her favourite. She complimented the dessert too. It was sherry trifle with jelly. Lord Clifford explained that he was lucky to have a fantastic chef, whom he had brought there from London. Louise again had an opportunity to talk about food. This time she told them about the recipe book she got from a French chef she had met on a visit to Paris. She couldn't remember his name, but he was very famous at that time. Oliver and Molly were quiet for the rest of dinner. When it was over, all the guests moved back into the drawing room where Oliver tried to talk to his father. Lord Clifford was now gloomy and unhappy and, as had been made clear over dinner, the fact that Oliver had brought Molly along had created some tension between them. There was still no sign of James.

Grace thanked Lord Clifford for a wonderful dinner, then made her excuses before leaving him to talk to her grandmother. She went over to Molly, hoping to lead her to the corner of the room so they could speak in private. At that moment Oliver approached them.

"My nieces tried to impress me with their French, thanks to Molly." He gave Molly a cheeky look.

"I always knew Molly had many talents." Grace caught herself being sarcastic but couldn't help it. The double meaning of her comment was understood by Molly only, who blushed.

"May I steal Molly away from you for a moment?" said Oliver, looking at Grace. And with that, the two of them left the room.

"Grace," said Louise, coming towards her. "You look fabulous. I really like your dress. It appears to have been specially made for you, am I right?"

"Thank you, Louise. You are right. It was made by my nana's seamstress."

"I knew it. Perhaps I will ask your grandmother for her contact details later." And without a pause, she took Grace's hand in hers and changed the subject.

"Grace, you must play the piano, right? Your beautiful fingers are just made for it." She started rubbing Grace's fingers.

"Yes, Louise," said Grace, extracting her hand as quickly as she could. "I love to play." She was still trying to make up her mind about Louise. She had mixed feelings about her, perhaps because of Molly. Louise moved a little closer.

"I know that Lord Clifford is very fond of listening to the piano." Then she turned and gazed at the instrument by the window in the corner of the room. "Would you mind playing something for us?"

Grace turned her head towards Lord Clifford. "I don't know …"

"Leave it with me." Louise crossed the floor to her brother and began to whisper in his ear. Lord Clifford glanced over at Grace and smiled. Seeing that Grace still hesitated, Lord Clifford and Louise walked to the piano and gestured for her to join them.

As soon as Grace's fingers touched the keys, the pleasant tune caught the attention of everyone in the room. They immediately fell silent and began to listen. Elizabeth looked very happy for her granddaughter and proud of her extraordinary ability. She moved closer and stood next to Lord Clifford. With wide eyes and a tilt of his head towards Grace, he indicated his surprise to Elizabeth and told her that he was impressed. Elizabeth nodded slightly in response and immediately raised her head up proudly. Everyone's attention was upon Grace who continued to play until she heard a slow clap from the door. They all turned to see … James. He stopped clapping and stood in the doorway swaying on his feet with one arm grasping the door frame. It was clear that he was drunk.

"Oh, he really is such an uncouth individual." Elizabeth couldn't stop making unpleasant comments that evening.

It was clear from the way Lord Clifford quickly walked over to James, and from his angry tone when he spoke to him, that it was time for the evening to end. Shortly, Louise and her family went upstairs to their rooms. As Molly was an unexpected guest, there was an awkward moment, no room had been made ready for her. That was sorted quickly, as Lord Clifford's attention was mostly on James at that time. He asked his housekeeper to show Molly the room where she could stay overnight. Elizabeth and Grace had been invited to stay for a few days and had arrived the day before, so they already knew their way and hurried to their rooms as well. Oliver, James and their father stayed in the drawing room.

Lying in bed, Grace listened to the loud voices from downstairs. It seemed to take forever before they stopped and she was able to fall asleep, plagued by thought, *who is this "James"?*

James Clifford

A rough diamond

Grace woke up before everyone else, feeling thirsty. The house was quiet. She carefully walked down the corridor, trying not to wake anybody. Heading towards the kitchen, she passed a room with a door half open. Unable to resist, she went inside to discover it was a library. Grace was instantly overpowered by the aroma of musty old books and mahogany wood. A bookcase filled with books from floor to ceiling covered an entire wall. She had never seen such a huge collection.

Choosing one, Grace sat on the sofa and flipped through the pages. It was *Pride and Prejudice* by Jane Austen; the book she had given away to Molly. She was glad to find it and hoped she would have the chance to read it to the end this time. She was so engrossed in reading that she didn't notice the time passing until the clock struck eight. She would have to be ready for breakfast soon. Grace snapped the book shut and got up hurriedly. She didn't notice James until she collided with him in the doorway.

"Oh, I'm terribly sorry." Grace froze in front of him.

James rubbed his eyes and yawned, all the while keeping his gaze on her face. In particular, he was staring at her lips, which she realised must be red and swollen. Grace had a habit of biting her lips while reading. Before she had a chance to duck past him, he grabbed her arm and pulled her towards him. Grace angrily freed herself, but kept standing where she was.

Taking a proper look at him, she saw that he was casually dressed in an opennecked white shirt with sleeves rolled up his arms. His dark hair, partly grey and long at the front, had a fringe covering his forehead. His eyes were dark, though his squinting gave them a hard and unattractive quality. He sported a pencil moustache, which added to his arrogant demeanour and made Grace turn her head away. She didn't like men with moustaches, but at that moment her feelings were mixed. James was too close to her. Before she could change her mind about this man, Grace blurted out. "I didn't think anybody would be in the hallway at this early hour."

"Anybody? Hmm … what are *you* doing here?" James ran a hand through his hair, then looked directly into Grace's eyes.

She pulled her dressing gown more tightly around her.

"So, you're not actually a ghost, are you?"

"I'm sure I didn't mean to startle you. You are James, am I right? I'm Grace, Elizabeth's granddaughter."

"I know who you are."

Grace didn't know what to say to that. They looked at each other for a moment.

"Well. It's nice to meet you, James." Grace went to pass him again. But he put his hand out, leaving her with no choice but to shake it. When she did, he turned it around and kissed the back, laughing when she pulled it away so fast it was like it had never been in his hand.

"You can't blame me," he said. "I'm not used to seeing a halfnaked woman in my house this early in the morning."

"I'm hardly naked!" Grace pulled her dressing gown even tighter. "I thought that everyone was still sleeping and that no one would see me. I was thirsty and wanted to go to the kitchen for a drink. I tried to be quiet."

"You seem to have confused the kitchen with the library." James took the book from Grace's hand without asking. Turned it over and gave it back to her with a grin. "I'm also very thirsty. Follow me. I will show you the way, just in case you miss it again."

He started to walk away, leaving Grace behind. She wanted to refuse to go with him but felt it would be rude. After all, she was a guest in the house. So, she followed him along the hall, down the stairs, and into a kitchen which was in the basement. The Georgianstyle kitchen was quite large with wooden, creamcoloured cabinets. The countertop, on which the housekeeper was preparing breakfast, was made from dark brown wood. Sumptuous smells of baking enveloped the room. When they walked in, the housekeeper said, “Good morning,” and promptly left.

James seemed glad to see the kettle boiling on the stove. He made himself comfortable at the large wooden table in the middle of the room and pointed to a cupboard with several bottles.

“Get me one of those, won’t you.”

Grace couldn’t understand what he wanted from her and wondered if the word *please* had somehow escaped this man’s vocabulary or was never there. Putting her book down on the table, she walked closer to the cupboard.

“There are only bottles of gin and whiskey in here.”

“Did you expect to see jars of honey? Make me a strong tea and add some whiskey to it.” He put his head in his hands and complained of a headache. The grimaces on his face were hard to read. Did he really have a headache or was he just pretending?

Grace decided to make him his whiskey tea as quickly as she could and get back to her bedroom. Under his smirking gaze, she rinsed the teapot, made the tea, poured him a cup and added the whiskey. She put it on the table in front of him, then muttered an apology and said that it was time for her to go up to her room. Her book was in her hands again, but before she could turn away, James grabbed her hand.

"I don't like drinking tea alone and I remember that you were thirsty too, weren't you? Where's your cup? Sit next to me. Tell me, how was the evening yesterday? Sorry I was late and missed all the *fun*. Oliver announced his engagement, didn't he?"

James got down another cup from the shelf next to them and poured tea for Grace, while she stood there struck with amazement.

"What engagement?" She was no longer thinking about leaving. Her curiosity betrayed her. She regretted showing her weakness, but it was too late.

"I was hoping to learn more about it from you." James grabbed a biscuit from the jar on the table.

"I don't know anything." Her book went back on the table. She glanced down into the teacup in front of her, before taking it with both hands, pretending she was sipping tea. At the same time, she watched him, hoping the side of the cup would hide her eyes.

"So, Ollie managed to hide it from everyone. That's my brother! He is quiet and charming, but nobody knows him better than me. Ah, Ollie."

James took a sip of tea and mimicked her, watching her over the rim of the cup. Then he looked her up and down and took another sip of his tea. Grace, still standing next to the kitchen table, didn't move. The news of the engagement had thrown her. Oliver and Molly had only known each other for a month, and for most of the evening they had not spoken much.

"I knew it. Your friend didn't tell you either."

"I haven't seen her for a month, and yesterday we didn't have much time to talk."

"Are you making excuses for your friend or for yourself?"

Grace felt ready to sink into the ground. In front of her sat this halfdrunk, unshaven, headacheridden man who had made her serve him tea in the kitchen. He wasn't embarrassed that she was standing in front of him in her nightwear and a dressing gown. It was clear from his tone that he was used to being commanding. And now, on top of all of this, he had managed, after only meeting her minutes before, to hit her rawest nerve. She could feel her cheeks getting red.

"I have to go, enjoy your tea. Hope it's strong enough." She put her cup down and quickly began to leave.

"You don't get away that fast." James almost jumped to stop Grace, who was nearly at the door. He wrapped one arm around her waist and closed the door behind her with his other hand.

Grace stared disapprovingly into his eyes while she struggled to free herself from his strong arms. He only held her tighter, then pressed his lips to hers so fast and hard that Grace's whole body shuddered in surprise.

James then took a step back, continuing to hold her waist

with one hand. He looked at her with a sarcastic smirk and whispered in her ear, "Now, you also have a secret from your friend Molly."

"How dare you?" Grace raised her hand to slap James on the face, but he caught it. He pressed her hand to his chest.

"It looks like we will be the first to announce our engagement, right?" He spoke in a languid voice and laughed, throwing his head back. "It was your first kiss. You cannot deny it, and now you have no choice."

James narrowed his eyes and studied Grace's face. His lips twisted in another smirk. Only then did he slightly relax his grip on her. Grace managed to wriggle free from James, opened the door and ran as fast as her legs could carry her, with the skin on her face flaming. She kept running all the way back to her bedroom, luckily without meeting anyone along the way. Shame burned through her for the way she had behaved in the kitchen. It wasn't like her. *Why did I follow him? Why did I stay there when he asked me to stay? Why did I even listen to him?* Questions swirled around her head, as she searched for an answer.

Grace looked in the mirror and didn't recognise herself. She raised her hand to touch her lips and closed her eyes. It was her *first* kiss. How could he have known that? She didn't like James, she knew that. But, at the same time, she had felt sorry for him when he complained about his headache. There was something about him at that moment which made him look vulnerable. Then he had surprised her with the news about Molly. What did he even know about her relationship with Molly? And then, his odd offer to announce their engagement, which was obviously a joke, but why had she felt so embarrassed? Grace decided to freshen up and calm herself down.

When she arrived for breakfast, Grace assumed her grandmother would already be there seeing as she was late herself. But there was no sign of Elizabeth or anybody else. Grace was worried and went straight back to her grandmother's room. She found her white-faced and quiet in her bed.

"Nana, how are you feeling? I hope you are not still angry with me. You are looking very pale. What is it?" Grace clasped her grandmother's hand.

Elizabeth waved her other hand, as if to say it wasn't worth talking about, but Grace could see she was still angry. She could also see she wasn't well.

"I think we should ask Lord Clifford to call the doctor."

"Nonsense. I will be fine after a bit of rest. I am getting old, my dear, and staying that late after dinner took its toll on me."

She slept fitfully throughout the day. Grace stayed with her, until her grandmother woke before dinner and insisted that Grace should go downstairs.

Grace, entering the dining room, spotted James and tensed, but breathed a sigh of relief when she saw Lord Clifford at the table as well. She didn't want to be with James on her own again. Dinner passed quietly. Lord Clifford explained that his sister had left, and that he was upset that Oliver had to go as well. He didn't say why, but Grace knew. Oliver, as a gentleman, left together with Molly, who couldn't stay longer without Lord Clifford's invitation. Most of the conversation was between Lord Clifford and Grace. They discussed his collection of books and paintings, which adorned all the walls of the house. Lord Clifford was impressed by Grace's knowledge of art. He complimented her for having played the piano so well the evening before and said that his wife had also played well, that it had been her piano. James stiffened when Lord Clifford mentioned his wife, James's mother, but remained silent, though he did seem to be listening attentively, glancing at Grace every now and then. She couldn't wait until dinner was over and for the moment when she could go back to her room.

Visiting her grandmother the following morning Grace could see straight away that her health had deteriorated. She ran downstairs and called for Lord Clifford.

"We need a doctor, your grace," she told him. "Nana ... she's not well."

Against all odds

Temptation

The butler opened the heavy front doors of Lord Clifford's mansion. Grace entered the hall and slowly raised her gaze to the ceiling with its beautiful stucco work and huge crystal chandelier. She tried to take in the paintings that hung on the walls, inspecting each of them in an effort to learn the artists' names, but her mind was still back at the hospital where she had left her grandmother to have some tests done. She felt tired and lonely.

It was chilly in the hall, and it seemed to Grace, in that moment, all the beauty of this rich interior really only served to hide a deep loneliness within the family. She went to the kitchen, thinking maybe she would have tea alone, but the housekeeper was there. She offered Grace something to eat but Grace declined and instead decided to go out into the gardens. She left through the main door, turning around to see the house in the evening sun.

It looked magnificent. The red front door stood out against the mix of impressive Gothic and Georgian architecture. The evergreen thujas were proudly stationed in a row on both sides of a driveway towards the entrance of the house. Grace looked around the huge Clifford Estate and thought that she could easily get lost there. She started to walk slowly around the gardens. Dusk was approaching and the floral scent of late summer filled the air. The gardens were well maintained, every bush beautifully trimmed. But she couldn't feel any joy. She came across a gazebo and went to sit there, but as soon as she sat down, she felt the need to stand again, restless. She decided to get a closer look at the flowers and bushes before it got too dark.

She reached the largest area of the gardens, the Butterfly Garden. When she had walked around the gardens with Lord Clifford the other day, she learned that the Butterfly Garden had been created by his late wife, Lady Clifford, who had loved butterflies. There was a huge variety of flowers and shrubs. Lord Clifford especially loved the very rare exotic plants he had brought from India, proudly enjoying when guests complimented him on their unusual beauty. His favourite place was on the paved terrace at the corner of the house, under the shade of a huge pine tree. Grace appreciated seeing Lord Clifford's enthusiasm for his gardens, since she herself loved gardening very much too. That mutual interest connected them. Looking at and listening to Lord Clifford, Grace considered how she lacked such warm male attention in her life. Her father and grandfather had died before she was born and she only experienced her grandmother's supervision while growing up. Her grandmother also seemed happy in the company of Lord Clifford. He was the type of man who would put anyone at ease. Grace had noticed how gently and masterfully he had placed his hand under her grandmother's elbow when they walked towards the dining room the other night. Such touching gestures told her that he cared for her grandmother, and this pleased Grace. She could see that their relationship gave both of them joy.

With that thought, she went further into the gardens, examining each flower she passed. Startled by a rustling sound from behind a tree, she turned, and a shadow rose in front of her. Grace screamed. A large hand quickly covered her mouth. She began to struggle, but the strong hands didn't let go of her. And then he spoke. Although he whispered, she immediately recognised the already familiar languid voice.

"You like being in my arms, don't you? I will let you go if you promise not to scream."

Grace stopped struggling and James turned her around, still keeping one hand across her mouth, the other on her shoulder. With her eyes closed, Grace nodded, and she felt James's hand pull back from her mouth. But before she could say anything, he was kissing her.

It was different from the kiss in the kitchen the day before. Passionate and a little softer. He held her differently too, in a way that suggested gentleness, while at the same time making it impossible for Grace to break away from him. He seemed to know exactly what to do with an inexperienced woman like herself. She wondered how many women he had been with.

The heat from James's body passed to her. She could feel his heart and her own beating quickly, in unison. When he gently ran his hand down her back and up to her hair, she found herself wanting him to do it again. It was as though they were communicating with their bodies, that they didn't need words. He pressed himself to her, as he slowly backed her up against a tree. James's cedarwood scented cologne filled her nose and lungs when the kiss stopped and she dropped her head to rest against the side of his neck. She took a deep breath and looked around nervously, worried that someone saw them. With pleading eyes, she slowly detached herself from him and looked away.

"Don't worry, we are alone here. You don't need to be afraid of me."

This time James was serious, there was no smirk when he spoke. He stroked her hair. Grace lowered her eyes. She couldn't say or do anything. She was less afraid of him today, but at the same time she was embarrassed by what he had awakened in her.

"I thought you had gone back to London." She tried to divert his attention from kissing her again.

"My car broke down, and when I came back, I found out that you and your grandmother were in the hospital. I went there, but you had already left."

"You went to the hospital? Why?" Grace couldn't believe it.

"Why? I was worried about your grandmother."

Confused, she thanked James for his concern. He took her arm and led her deeper into the gardens, telling her there was something he wanted to show her. She let him lead her until a small stone house appeared in front of them, enveloped in greenery. He stopped.

"This is an old gate lodge. It has been abandoned for a long time My mother insisted on renovating it for me. I spent my best years in here with my mother, hiding from my father. Then she died …"

Grace could detect the love he had for his mother in his voice.

"I'm sorry, James. What age were you when your mother died?" asked Grace in her gentle voice.

"Nine," was the short answer.

James gestured for Grace to come into the lodge with him. He opened the door, which wasn't locked. She was surprised that its hinges didn't creak and that it was clean inside when they entered.

"Our housekeeper looks after it. She has worked for us since I was born. I only come to York because of this place. It's my refuge, and I only want *you* here with me."

Grace didn't know what to say.

Inside the lodge, there was one good-sized room with a sofa, table and two soft armchairs in it. She noticed a cobweb inside the small fireplace near the sofa, which seemed to have been out of use for years. Overall, the room was cosy and had the smell of dry herbs. A feeling of warmth and relaxation slowly filled her. While she was looking around, James crossed the room and closed the short cotton curtains on the windows. There was an old chest in the corner. James opened it and to her disbelief retrieved out a bottle of wine.

"The chest may be old, but this fine claret is possibly even older." James put the bottle on the table next to two glasses.

Without even looking at Grace, he also pulled out a bar of fine chocolate, which was a rare treat during wartime.

"James, where did you get all of this?" she asked, but in her head, she meant, *when did you get the time to bring wine and chocolate to the lodge, and why?*

"From this medieval magic chest." He thumped the box with his foot and laughed. She laughed with him, and the tension in the atmosphere went away.

After they had made themselves comfortable on the sofa, James told Grace a little bit about his childhood.

"You remind me of my mama when you laugh."

"Do I? I'll take that as a compliment."

"As I remember, she tried her best to show me that she was happy, but I don't think she was. When I was upset about something, she would do anything to make me laugh."

"Your mother was a real angel."

"She was. I will never forget her funeral. My life changed after that." At that moment, James suddenly moved towards the table where the bottle of wine and two glasses were. James uncorked the bottle and poured the wine into the two glasses. He turned back around to Grace and said, "There is something else that reminds me about my mama."

"What is it?"

"She liked red wine and this was one of her favourites, a 1918 Haut Brion." James passed one glass, filled up almost to the top, to Grace.

Grace hadn't expected such frankness from him, and through this, he won her trust. As they spoke, they drank wine. In his eyes, Grace could see how James had suffered from the loss of his mother at such a young age. It seemed that this pain was still deep in his heart. And she noticed how much he hated his father, blaming him for his mother's death.

He also clearly resented the fact that his father had sent him away to boarding school with its strict rules and tasteless meals, as he described it. After his mother died, James and his father had hardly spent any time together, but according to James he had not missed his father, a hint of bitterness in his voice as he spoke. It was only when James turned the conversation to Oliver that his face lit up. Strangely, the fact that Oliver was his father's favourite son didn't seem to have affected the relationship between the brothers. It was clear James trusted Oliver, that he felt sure his younger brother would always support him and protect him from his father. Grace wondered if, maybe, Oliver felt guilty for getting more of his father's attention. And perhaps because their mother had died when Oliver was very young, it hadn't affected him in the same way as James.

Then Grace told James about her childhood. About how grateful she was to her grandmother for everything. About how she often thought of her parents in Ireland, who had died so young. How she loved horses and drawing. Hearing this, James promised to take her to the races one day. They hardly noticed as the time flew by, and they felt good and comfortable on the sofa in front of the unlit fireplace. The wine relaxed Grace – perhaps too much. When James covered her shoulders with a blanket, she snuggled into him. Then he gently hugged and kissed her.

It was as if time paused. But after a moment of hesitation, Grace threw her arms around James's neck and kissed him back. She realised that she was giving him permission to lead her into a new and unknown world. Grace felt like she was drunk, but she wasn't sure if it was from the wine or from her new feelings. She and James had a strong emotional connection; there was an intense chemistry between them. It was euphoric and exhilarating. The kiss went on far too long and it overwhelmed her. James's hands were, by that time, all over her body.

"James …" Grace was out of breath. "Too fast …"

"I can stop." He started kissing the side of her neck gently, holding her hair out of the way.

"Yes … No … I mean …" Grace's thoughts were confused. She felt the heat from his lips on her skin and was losing herself.

"So, yes or no?" James asked, kissing her again, this time slowly moving down her shoulder and chest.

Grace wasn't able to think and kiss him at the same time. His hand moved down her leg. She pushed him away and tried to catch her breath.

"Let me show you this beautiful world. Its only you and me here. You can trust me. You smell of *honey*. Umm … delicious and irresistible. You are so sweet." James's hoarse voice ignited fireworks of unknown feelings in Grace, burning her sense of reality.

After another passionate kiss, they somehow ended up under the blankets, naked. Grace was embarrassed by her body, but

James's skilful caresses reassured her. When Grace stopped for a second, in doubt, James quickly showed her the way to move, teaching her how to make love. He was patient with her, but he was moving so fast that she didn't have time to stop him. He took her further and deeper into a whirlpool of passion, which she unexpectedly revelled in, struck by the forbidden thought that she liked it. A quick, almost unnoticed, pain was forgotten in a second: this first, one she would remember all her life. They made passionate love all night. She couldn't remember when the flames inside her finally extinguished and her body, damp with sweat and smelling of cedarwood, was left lying contentedly.

A ray of early morning sunlight crept through the narrow gap in the curtains and gently touched Grace's face. She woke up, still in the lodge, to find James wasn't with her. She raised her head from the cushion and looked around the room in which her life had taken a new direction. An awkward sensation slowly rose inside her. Now sober, she was overcome with shame. What *had* she done? Trusting a man, she barely knew, like that. A man like James Clifford, of all people. Grace thought of her grandmother. About how she had brought Grace up to understand and obey strict rules of behaviour concerning men, including that the first man Grace was intimate with should be her *husband*. Everything had happened so fast.

Grace closed her eyes for a moment and let herself recall James's sweet embrace. A wave of dizziness hit her. Did it really happen? When she tried to get up, she knew straight away that, yes, it *did*. Her body told her so. She closed her eyes again and stood in the middle of the room for another moment. She couldn't believe that she had allowed James to take control over her. How could she throw caution to the wind? Her heart roared with indignation.

She dressed quickly and returned to the mansion in hope of catching James there. He was nowhere to be found. The housekeeper hadn't seen him either. He had simply disappeared. Once he'd had his way, she was forgotten. A flash of realisation hit her: he might have just been playing with her. *What kind of man is he?* Grace paced her bedroom floor, not stopping until one of the maids knocked on her door. The car was ready to take Grace back to the hospital to visit her grandmother.

Nana

Last goodbye

It had been a difficult month. The journey home from Lord Clifford's estate had been long and arduous on her grandmother. Instead of improving, as the hospital doctor had told Grace she might, Elizabeth had grown steadily worse. She had taken to her bed that first day she had arrived home and had essentially stayed there all the time since. In the rare moments where she seemed to have gathered some strength, all she wanted to do was to talk to her lawyer, to get her affairs in order. There had been so much running around. Then, in the evenings, there would be a deathly silence, so that Elizabeth could rest and sleep.

Grace was exhausted. Though she had assistance from the house staff, in particular one of the maids, and the family doctor regularly called, she had felt alone that whole, long month caring for her very ill grandmother. And she was ashamed that, despite the gravity of her grandmother's situation, her thoughts kept returning to James, who never once wrote to her or called, and who didn't accompany Lord Clifford and Oliver the time they paid a visit.

"Molly is worried about you," Oliver said, smiling nervously. "I think she was trying to get hold of you."

"She called. Thanks, Oliver," was Grace's short reply.

She knew she sounded curt, but she couldn't help it. Just like she hadn't been able to help being rude to Molly, telling her she didn't need any assistance. One part of her would have loved nothing more than the company and support of her old friend. Another part wanted never to see her again. Would her grandmother have fallen ill, had she not received such a shock, seeing Molly arrive at the dinner party with Oliver?

There was a moment when Elizabeth gathered some strength back and wanted to talk to Grace.

"My dear Grace, my beautiful granddaughter. Why are you so sad? There is no need for that." Grace quickly pulled herself together and curved her lips into a soft smile.

"How are you feeling, Nana? Do you need anything?"

"I have already had everything in this life, thank you, sweetheart. Now I want *you* to have a good life no matter what obstacles you encounter. Be brave, but be careful. Please let Lord Clifford help you when I am gone. All right?"

"Nana, please. I need you and will do anything for you to get better."

"You have to let me go. But before I go … yes, you can do something for me. I want you to promise me that you will get married as soon as possible. Unfortunately, I cannot help you with that anymore, but you can rely on Lord Clifford. You will need help to manage the estate. My lawyer will explain everything. You must not worry, you will have enough for living, but … you need a husband. Especially now, when the world is shaking and there is chaos in the country. It is not safe to live on your own. A young lady like you …" Elizabeth sounded out of breath.

"All right, Nana, all right. I understand. Please keep your energy, and rest. I promise I will do my best to make you happy."

"Good. But you need to make your future *husband* happy. I will tell you a little secret …"

"Nana, I would love to know your secret, but maybe later? You look pale."

"I am all right, my dear." After a short pause she continued, "You must know that I was not in love with your grandfather. It was an arranged marriage. And it worked. So, remember that! We respected each other and love came later."

"But what if love won't come?"

"It depends on what your expectations of love are. It has many shades. I raised you to be strong and learn how to control your emotions. If you let them run like wild horses, you will lose the race."

"I will listen to my heart, Nana."

"Oh, do not invite troubles, my dear. You do not need drama

which will ruin your life. While you listen to your heart, others will use their brains."

The message was very direct, even without her nana knowing what had happened at the gate lodge. It was clear to Grace that she had used her heart that night, not her brain. But, this time, she wasn't offended by her grandmother's remarks, and leaned over to her. "Nana, I think you are getting better. And if you really want to see me married, you must be at my wedding!"

"I wish, my dear, I wish … You are an intelligent girl, but delicate. I trust you to do the right thing." Elizabeth let out a weak sigh.

Grace held her grandmother's hand in hers, feeling its warmth. "I love you, Nana," she said, but her grandmother had already closed her eyes and probably didn't hear her. That was the last time Elizabeth Bellmore spoke.

Grace was with her grandmother when she quietly left this world. It was just the two of them in the vast bedroom of their home in White Cliffs. The maid had gone downstairs to make supper. Elizabeth had been sleeping fitfully all day. Then, her breathing changed. When Grace leaned over to check if she was comfortable, her breathing stopped altogether. Grace felt as though her world had collapsed. She was twenty-one years of age the day her grandmother died and she felt terribly alone.

After crying a lot, she went to the window and looked out at the garden. It felt impossible – the idea of White Cliffs without her beloved nana. She wasn't ready for life on her own. And the idea came to her that if it turned out that Molly and Oliver weren't actually together and Oliver would consider proposing to Grace, then she would accept. Yes, she would – to honour her grandmother.

"Nana, I would do anything to bring you back. I love you and miss you already so much!" Tears rolled down Grace's cheeks before she remembered that her grandmother didn't like her crying, so she swiped them away with shaking fingers.

Sunset on the beach

Time to make a decision

Following the gloomy, rainy night, it was exceptionally warm that day. This gave Grace the opportunity to walk down from White Cliffs to the beach. The fresh salty breeze greeted her straight away. Grace took off her shoes and continued to walk towards the sea. The warmth of the sun was still in the sand. She removed the pin from her hair and let the wind play with it. Shading her eyes against a strong ray of evening light, she gazed at the horizon where the sun was slowly dropping.

It had been a month since her grandmother's funeral. Grace had found it particularly hard to accept peoples' condolences and to talk to the family lawyer. James hadn't even shown up. Molly had come, but Grace was cold to her, pretending not to have heard when Molly suggested she could stay with her for a few days. At least it seemed that there was little left for her to do in terms of paperwork. Her grandmother had left things in good order, probably because she had known she wasn't long for this world. After the funeral, Lord Clifford had told Grace that Elizabeth had even discussed with him how to help Grace after she was gone. More than anything, this made Grace sad.

Lord Clifford had also offered his help and invited her to stay at the Clifford Estate, mentioning some outstanding affairs he had to discuss with her related to the Bellmore horse business. There was money owed to Grace from the sale of some horses. She had politely declined his offer and promised to speak to him later. She was tired of other people, walking around, offering help. The only person she wanted to see had never appeared. Now she wanted nothing more than to be left alone.

It felt good to be on the beach. Usually, she went there almost daily when she was in White Cliffs, but she hadn't been at all over the past month. She took off her cardigan and let it fall to the sand. The early autumn wind instantly cooled the skin on her arms, as she was in a sleeveless dress. On impulse, she ran into the sea, the water covering first her feet, then her knees, then above, the splashes hitting her face. She stopped when the water came halfway up her body. Then she stood there, eyes closed, hands clenched into fists under the surface, her whole body was tense from the cold. The thought flashed through her mind to plunge into the sea and wash away all her worries, her fears, her anger, but something stopped her – probably the temperature.

Grace opened her eyes. The horizon was illuminated by

a beautiful sunset. The sun hadn't yet set, but the sky was splashed with red and yellow colours. Grace stared up at the view, spellbound. A sharp shiver ran down her legs and she realised that she was freezing. She quickly got out of the sea, picked up her cardigan and put it over her shoulders. Her feet were pleased to be in the warm sand again. Slowly, her body started to heat up. Grace decided to sit on a rock to watch the sunset before she went home. She felt a little refreshed.

Distant memories of her childhood came to her. She couldn't remember her mother, but she often imagined how they would walk together along the white sandy beach in Donegal. They would play on the shore, then watch the waves and listen to the seagulls. Grace had always loved the sea. She cried, not just for her grandmother, but now also for her mother, whom she missed dearly.

Back at the house, the housekeeper came out to greet her. There had been a call while she was down at the beach. Lord Clifford had invited her to come to his birthday dinner the following week. Grace didn't know what to do. On the one hand, she didn't want to risk encountering James, because she was angry with him. On the other, it was clear that she couldn't keep refusing Lord Clifford's invitations. He was always so kind to her, constantly offering her his support, and she knew if she stayed alone in the house for longer, she would get depressed. Encountering James might at least lead to some answers. That incomprehensible and volatile man, whom she disapproved of so much, for some reason still occupied her mind. She looked out the window, back towards the sea.

In good times and bad, the sea had always been there for her, like a medicine, relaxing her when she was stressed, or recharging her with a new energy when she needed it. For now, it had helped Grace to clear her mind for a moment.

"I will go," she said to herself. "I will go and see what happens."

Shocking surprise

A cryptic ring

When Grace arrived at Lord Clifford's estate, Molly was already there, sitting on the sofa beside Oliver, a teacup held daintily in her hand. Her little finger was extended, as though she herself had been raised in a mansion. It didn't surprise Grace, the fact that Molly was there. Though they hadn't spoken about Oliver since Lord Clifford's last dinner, she had no reason to think that things were over between them. On the contrary, at her grandmother's funeral, she had noticed Oliver placing his hand on Molly's back as he led her to his car. It wasn't as though she had any reason to be annoyed with Molly. Especially after what had happened with James. Now Grace was the one keeping a secret.

Grace sat beside her friend. She even managed to smile at her. Molly smiled back warmly after they had said hello to each other and then descended into silence. Maybe Grace's coolness towards her was now making her cautious. Maybe she was worried she would say the wrong thing about Grace's grandmother. Some people, Grace had learned, didn't know what to say to someone who was grieving, so much so that they would say nothing at all. She understood, but it didn't mean she had to sit in awkward silence with Molly and Oliver until dinner.

It was lovely out in the garden where Grace preferred to be. A soft, warm breeze woke up the fragrances of all the flowers and the scent of freshly cut grass. Birds were singing, the bees were still buzzing in that lovely September evening. Sitting on a bench, she felt herself almost relax. It had been such a difficult last two months. On top of caring for her grandmother and the pain of grief, she had been worried that she might be pregnant. At least, since yesterday, she didn't have that to worry about. It felt strange, being there in the same garden where she had let herself be taken by James. Heat rose in her face just thinking about it. Maybe no one would marry her now her reputation was soiled.

This thought had just crossed her mind when the sound of someone walking startled her. She looked up, and to her astonishment and confusion, saw James, standing right there. He might have dominated her thoughts for the last month, but now that he was in front of her, she only felt confused, and she knew the risk of meeting him here.

"Grace," he whispered softly.

"Please, James, don't." Grace stretched out her arm, as though to keep him at bay.

"How are you?" He came closer to her.

"Please leave me alone."

"I had to go away on business."

"I understand, there is no need for excuses."

"That was not an excuse. I couldn't come to the funeral, but I was thinking about you. That's what I wanted to say."

"Good that you didn't come."

"Look, I think we need to talk."

"No, we don't."

"I understand you are upset, but I will try to explain everything. Give me a chance."

"*What* do you need to explain?" Grace could feel her emotions starting to betray her. *Hold your horses!* she said to herself.

"No need to raise your voice. Pretty girls don't shout, do they? You can say whatever you feel you want to say, but let me speak as well. It was … I wanted …"

To her surprise, he seemed to be struggling to find the right words. But she wouldn't let herself be charmed a second time. Grace stood and began to walk away.

"Damn this girl!" he said under his breath. She heard him, but for some reason pretended that she hadn't.

"Grace, wait!"

"Stop following me."

Not only had he followed her, he had also managed to guide

her in the wrong direction, she realised: away from the house.

"I want to go back to the house." Her voice was weak.

"Look, Grace. I'm sorry. All right, I said it! The reason I wasn't at your grandmother's funeral was because I have hated funerals ever since my mama died."

Oh, no! Why on earth would he mention his mother now? He looked so vulnerable, standing there. Like a child. If he was acting, he was very good at it. She struggled with her feelings.

"I'm not the type to get on my knees and beg. Please don't make me …"

It occurred to Grace that if she pushed him away now, she would lose him forever. She had to think quickly. She had to think of her reputation. Her head was spinning. She felt lost. She didn't know how she would manage the house and the business, all left to her in her grandmother's Will. It was too much. It seemed as though she still had a chance with James after all. Not only that, but the way he was holding back as best as he could right now… It wasn't his style to ask for forgiveness. He was trying his best to find the right words. It was so disarming. How could she turn him away? And hadn't her grandmother always taught her to be polite to those who were offensive to her?

Grace straightened her back and took a deep breath.

"James, I don't want to talk about what happened. It is your father's birthday today."

"You are my joy! And so right. Finally, we can resume a civil conversation between us." James kissed the back of Grace's hands. And the conversation slipped back into the tone they had used at the gate lodge. "Come with me, I will show you something."

"James, please. No more surprises. And it's getting late."

"You will like it, I promise. We will be back well before dinner."

Grace had not realised there was a lake on the estate. And yet there it was, at the end of a large field, many metres wide, adorned with water lilies at its edge, and only a fiveminute walk from where she had encountered James. She couldn't help smiling when she took it in. And when she felt his gaze on her, and his pleasure at her pleasure, she could only smile more.

"Swans, white swans. They are so beautiful." She pointed to the pair who had just made their elegant way into view.

"Your eyes are literally sparkling." He put his hand on her shoulder.

"You know that swans choose a partner for life." Grace didn't look at James as she said this.

"Yes? So that is why they always appear in a pair."

"Do you believe that people can do the same?"

"Hmm, if you turn into a swan, then I will be with you forever."

Grace smiled, looking down at the lake. Obviously, it was a joke.

"And now … I will turn you into a swan."

Before she even had a chance to figure out what he meant by this, James leaned in and planted his lips lightly on Grace's, his hands resting on her shoulders. It was only for a moment and then he pulled back, gazing quizzically at her, a smile hovering on his mouth. It was at that moment it hit her – how lonely she had been. Maybe she had always been lonely. Lonely and yet so full of love. And now here was a man, standing in front of her, offering his love to her. She leaned in to return his kiss and this time they kissed for longer, his arms tight and protective around her back. She had nothing to lose anymore. Part of her was still angry that she was letting him kiss her like this, after not having heard from him in so long. Another part of her felt a sweet relief. Like she had been waiting all her life for this. She thought at that moment she loved him, and it seemed, his returning to her was proof that he loved her too.

There was a lively atmosphere at dinner. Lord Clifford was in good spirits. It was clear to Grace, even though no one told her as much, that he now approved of Oliver's relationship with Molly. She found herself wondering if this was easier for him now that her grandmother was gone. Maybe he had found it hard to stand up to her. Oliver wouldn't have had to try that hard. Molly was bright and friendly; Grace had to admit that. Still, she was glad when James invited her to sit beside him at the table. It made her feel like she wasn't alone anymore.

"That pair seem to be very close these days," James whispered, gesturing towards Oliver and Molly. "Shall we call them Ollie-Molly?" He couldn't hide his laugh.

Grace replied in a cheeky tone, "I wonder if Oliver is going to announce their engagement this time?"

James looked at her closely. Then his expression changed in a way that made her feel vaguely alarmed.

"What?"

He winked at her.

"What is it?"

"It is not all about them, you know."

"What do you mean?"

"Maybe someone else will get there first."

Before she had a chance to answer, and just as Oliver stood, his glass raised, James jumped to his feet.

"Oliver. You might let me, as your older brother, be the first to give a toast."

"Yes, of course, James. Go ahead." Oliver sat back in his seat.

"Firstly, I want to wish my father a happy birthday." James raised his glass without even turning towards his father.

Everyone at the table stared at James. Louise and her husband had a look on their faces like something terrible was going to happen. Their daughters waited impatiently, whispering into each other's ears.

"And I have a present for him," continued James.

Lord Clifford's smile flickered off his face.

James reached into the right pocket of his jacket and pulled out a good-sized oval ruby ring. It sparkled in the lamplight and everyone gasped.

"Grace, this ring belonged to my mama. It was very dear to her and is very dear to me." He glanced at his father. "You probably don't remember, but mama bought it in India and loved it."

Lord Clifford cleared his throat. "Of course, I remember it, James."

"Grace, sweetheart. Will you be my wife?"

"Oh my, oh my," was Molly's reaction. She looked at Grace and the surprise on her face was a reflection of Grace's own.

Grace froze in momentary shock. She was not prepared for this. Her thoughts were moving so fast she felt they would reach the moon and back in a fleeting second. Her grandmother's words and wishes, the fact she lost her head at the gate lodge two months ago, and other hidden truths, flew through her mind. *Do I want to marry him?* It was hard at that moment to listen to her heart and use her brain. She felt like they were opponents on a battlefield, fighting for the right answer.

"Yes … James." Still in shock, she managed to look in his eyes. With her gaze, she attempted to travel, as deep as possible, inside his soul to see his true feelings for her. But she couldn't find an answer there, or she simply didn't have enough time. Grace watched James putting his mother's ring on her finger. At least his smile went all the way to his eyes. In that moment her life deviated from its expected course.

"There is not going to be a big wedding or anything. Just a quick affair before we head to India. That's right. My betrothed will be accompanying me on my return. Which means that we need to settle all the formalities before leaving." With that proudly said, James turned to Grace, grinning at her. She stood next to him and tried to understand what had just happened.

Looking down at the ring on her finger, she murmured, "It has an unearthly beauty." She felt everyone's eyes on her, and wondered if they thought her voice sounded strange. "It's a great privilege," she managed to continue, "to wear your mother's ring, James." As she spoke, to her surprise, tears welled up in her eyes. James gave her a light kiss in front of everyone.

Then they all began offering their congratulations.

"You know how to surprise, James," said Lord Clifford, after everyone else had spoken.

"Indeed, I do, Father."

"Congratulations to both of you!"

Grace noticed Lord Clifford's concerned expression, but then it changed quickly and he nodded as he congratulated her. He was always so kind. Perhaps he was upset that James, not Oliver, would be marrying her. Maybe she was wrong and there was another reason. She simply didn't have time to figure it out then.

Grace watched Lord Clifford nod discreetly at a servant, who began to refill everyone's glasses. Dinner resumed, the birthday celebration turned into a celebration of James and Grace's engagement. The dining room was filled with the smell of roasted meat, vegetables and wine, the sound of cutlery, and conversation about daily routines during wartime. She couldn't wait until it came to an end. After they had retired to the drawing room, as soon as she felt it wouldn't be impolite, she made her excuses and went to her bedroom, claiming she had a headache. She went first to the kitchen to arrange for a tray with tea to be brought to her room. On the way back, as she was passing the library, she slowed down overhearing James's angry voice.

"You will say nothing to her!"

"She is your wife-to-be and has the right to know," replied Lord Clifford.

"It is not *your* business to instruct me what to tell *my* wife."

"All right. All right, James. I just thought …"

"Think for yourself, Father. Never mention it again!"

Grace rushed to her room. *What was that about?* James and his father were clearly speaking about her. There was something he didn't want her to know. Whatever it was, it made James very angry. She didn't want to start her marriage knowing her husband was keeping secrets from her, but maybe James just wanted to tell her himself and not let his father do so. She thought it would be best to wait and see. There was too much on her mind already.

Grace knew it was Molly straight away when, a few minutes later, there came a timid knock on her bedroom door. For a while, the two friends sat in silence. Then Molly spoke.

"Grace, I'm very happy for you," she said quickly. "It's so unexpected, but I'm really glad. What a surprise!" She glanced over at Grace.

"Thanks, Molly. I thought you liked surprises." Grace nervously started to move things around in the room.

"I have to say all of us were astounded. I didn't know you two were an item. When did it happen?"

Grace tilted her head. "Really? You want me to tell you everything when you wouldn't do the same. That's too much, Molly."

"I see you are still angry with me. I don't blame you."

"Why would I be angry with you?"

"I'm sorry I didn't tell you about me and Oliver. I should

have, I know. But I didn't know how or what to say to you. I decided to wait until I knew about Oliver for sure. Then he invited me to join him for that dinner. I didn't have a chance to talk to you beforehand."

"The dinner *I* told you about." Grace raised her eyebrows at Molly. "And, I also helped you to get *that* job through which you met Oliver in the first place."

"I know, and I am so grateful to you, Grace. You might not believe me, but I am," said Molly miserably.

"Yet you still couldn't find time to tell me."

Grace couldn't keep her feelings to herself anymore. What hurt wasn't the fact that Molly and Oliver had got together, but that Molly had kept it a secret, and that seeing the two of them arrive together for that dinner had shocked her grandmother so badly.

"Everything happened so fast. I'm sorry, Grace. You weren't interested in Oliver. I didn't know you would react like that."

"You and Oliver …" Grace struggled to find words. "Nana might not have died if …"

"Please Grace … don't say that, it's not true. Would you have married Oliver against your wishes to satisfy your grandmother?"

Grace took a deep breath, then replied, "The fact that you are with Oliver is of little interest to me, but why hide it? Nana was very upset that day because of what you did."

"Grace, I'm really sorry, I didn't mean to. I didn't know. It was Oliver who offered to take me with him to dinner. Let's not talk about this now. Today is your special day, full of happiness. Please enjoy it."

"Happiness ..." Grace repeated the word without knowing she was going to, or why.

"Oliver and I also had news for everyone, you know."

"News? What news?" *Again!* Grace blamed herself silently as her emotions took over.

"Oliver proposed to me. We are engaged to be married too. We were going to announce it at dinner, but you two beat us to it." Molly tried to smile.

Hearing this Grace felt satisfied. At least she had done something before her friend did. She didn't return Molly's smile, asking, "Lord Clifford didn't mind?"

"Well. He didn't, but he has arranged for me to have a medical checkup with their family doctor. Would you believe that?!"

"What? Tell me you are joking."

"I'm serious! Oliver Clifford can't marry someone without assurances she can help him continue the family name. I have one task, and that is to give birth to a healthy heir." Molly affected Lord Clifford's voice and despite herself, Grace laughed. Their affection for each other had been restored.

"He is not the worst," said Grace.

"I actually like him. I don't think he is a snob."

"Me neither."

"Someone said to me that 'new money' people are often worse snobs than 'old money' but it's not true with him."

"So, you too then. All right, Molly, congratulations!" Grace gave her friend a long hug.

"Do you remember," said Molly, "when we were young…"

Grace finished for her. "We wanted to marry brothers. Yes, I remember. We were so naive."

"Looks like dreams can come true in the end."

"They do indeed, even when you least expect it."

"Are you all right, Grace? You seem upset."

"I'm fine. Just a lot to think about."

"You know you can talk to me, any time."

"I know that. It's just that the war is getting to me."

"It's hard to be happy, isn't it? Knowing so many are risking their lives and so many will lose them. When your life could be over at any second, how can it be right to be happy?"

To Grace's surprise, she saw her friend's eyes were wet with tears.

"Oh, Molly. Your brother. I'm sorry, I wasn't thinking."

Molly shook her head, but tears were spilling down her cheeks.

"My good, true friend. Molly."

That evening, as they hugged each other and cried together,

it brought them closer than their childhood friendship. Grace then told Molly everything. She couldn't hold it back from Molly anymore. About that night in the gate lodge, about the carelessness that could ruin her reputation, and about how she was hurt. About the fact that she hadn't known she was getting married until James proposed to her at dinner and announced it to everyone. About her mixed feelings for James, and her fears.

Molly, in return, told Grace about Oliver. From these shared stories, they both learned more about the brothers and, while Molly wanted to get married as soon as possible, Grace was afraid.

"What are your doubts?"

"Everything happened so quickly. I don't really know James."

"My mother says a girl is not obliged to know her husband before marriage. She has her whole life ahead of her for that. In any case, a man always changes when he becomes a husband. What is the point in bothering to get to know him beforehand if he's going to change anyway?"

"It does make sense. Your mother is right, Molly."

"A waste of time, that is all it would be. The main thing is that a man can provide for his wife and children. And is that not the important thing to us women, to feel safe? That our husbands' jobs are to take care of our families?"

“Feeling safe, I agree, is important.”

“Grace, you have a big dowry. You shouldn’t worry at all.”

“That reminds me, I need to meet with a lawyer about Nana’s Will. So many things are going to pile on me soon, I’m afraid to even think about it.”

“You don’t have to, because now you have James. He will help you. Remember you once told me everything happens when it needs to happen.”

“I remember, Molly. That’s right. But I have to tell you, I am immensely frightened. It’s so far away. I have never travelled outside England. Promise you will come to India as well. Promise?”

“I promise. Of course I will come. Oliver said as soon as we are married we will start making plans about India.”

“I wish we could stay here for a while so I could be there for your wedding. Why does he have to be in such a hurry to get back to India?”

“I wouldn’t worry about it. He has his duty. I would like you to be at my wedding too. I wish we could have two weddings on the same day, but … I know some wives stay behind when their husbands go to serve in India and join them later. I think you had better go with your husband. It seems James is the type of man who wouldn’t like to leave his wife behind. In a way, it’s not a bad sign.” Molly winked at her.

“I’m so scared. What will it be like over there? I know

nothing about India apart from a few stories of Nana's, who told me that the life there was dysfunctional."

"And I heard different stories. Don't dwell on it too much. It will be wonderful. I bet there is a lovely place for you to live. Oh, and what about your honeymoon?"

"James told me that the life in India will be my extended honeymoon."

"I guess … he knows better. Lots of servants. Beautiful gardens. You won't want for anything. Who knows, you might fall in love with your new life out there and won't wish to come back."

"So fast. Everything's happened so fast … I can't recognise myself and feel like I am delirious, as if I have been poisoned."

"Well, use your antidotes then." Molly grabbed Grace's hand and looked in her eyes adoringly. "Love … they say love is the best antidote!"

Part II

India 1943–1947

Journey into the unknown

Escaping danger

Up on deck of the ship that was taking Grace and James to India, the air was salty and clean. Finally, after days of terror, the passengers were allowed out of their cabins. The ship had to run the gauntlet of German U-boats which were actively patrolling the French Atlantic coast. Grace leaned over the edge of the ship and stared at the horizon. The shores of England could no longer be seen. What she would have given to have the ship turn around and sail her home to White Cliffs.

At this stage she had stopped looking for her husband. As soon as they had got on board and were settled in their cabin, he disappeared to the bar whenever it opened. Grace stayed outside for a while until the chilly sea air started to bite. Her skin felt coated with sea salt. She decided to walk back to their cabin, but then saw her husband throwing up over the side of the ship, so she rushed to him.

"James, are you alright?"

"Dammit. What are *you* doing here? I'm fine." He quickly put a small bottle of whiskey in his pocket and gave Grace an angry look.

"I'm … I just couldn't stay in the cabin on my own," she said in hope he would come back there with her. She tried to move closer to him, but he started to walk faster.

"Do you need to follow me? Read a book, drink tea or something else, just don't check on me."

"I'm not checking on you. I came out for some fresh air. Do you know how many more days we have of the journey?"

"Soon. We will be there soon." Then he turned around, and walking backwards, shouted, "Don't get sick. Go back to the cabin!" and disappeared behind one of the side doors on the promenade deck.

Grace closed her eyes and said a little prayer that she would get to the shores of India as soon as possible, safe and sound. Even as she was whispering the words, her mind returned to her wedding night. Not for the first time, she regretted not telling Molly about it. Her nononsense, practical wisdom would have shooed away Grace's silly concerns. At the time, she had a vague sense that it would be disloyal to her new husband to tell Molly, but now that seemed a pointless concern. But she did still feel guilty. Even though, surely, it wasn't her fault, the way things had happened. After all, their wedding night wasn't the first time they had been together, but James changed after the wedding. For some reason he was angry with her back on their wedding night, and he was still angry. *What did I do wrong?*

Arrival in Calcutta, India

Mixed feelings

After a long, gruelling journey from Bombay, Grace and James arrived at their house in Calcutta. It was October of 1943 and the air was dry. While they had been in the car, she had learned from James about the Indian weather. Calcutta was located only twenty feet above sea level and was at risk of flooding in heavy rain. The monsoon season had passed and the heat would not return until March. James prepared her for the need to adjust to the Indian climate, saying that they had arrived at a good time and that winter would be the best season, with its desirable dry and cool air.

The house was a bungalow with a covered multiporticoed porch at the front, typical of the style occupied by many of the British Raj. The fragrance of jasmine and orange blossoms reached her nose. A variety of marigolds beautifully framed the landscape in front of the house. James and Grace were greeted at the porch by a young Indian girl in her mid-twenties dressed in a full-length sari. She was short in stature and her dark, round brown eyes smiled at them. James started to say something but paused.

"Zia," the young woman said.

"That's right, yes, Zia." He turned to Grace. "She was just hired. I sent a telegram asking for a maid for you before we left England. She was recommended. So, I hope she's good." Then he addressed Zia again.

"Please let me introduce you to my wife, your mistress."

"Namaste, memsahib. Pleasure to serve you, memsahib." Zia bowed her head.

"Thank you, Zia."

"Namaste, sahib." She did the same to James.

"Where is that damn boy. Never around!" James said gruffly.

Grace saw a boy running towards them at the speed of a sprinter. He was probably the same age as Zia, skinny, but with strong arms and legs. When he reached them, he stood straight like a tree that had never experienced the wind. James pointed towards the car where the driver had already started to remove their luggage. The boy was gone in a second to help.

"This is your new home, darling," said James proudly when they walked in. She could hear that he was exhausted, but she noticed a spark in his eyes. It was obvious he was happy to be home, his home. And she could already pick up a change in his body language. Probably life was more comfortable for him in India than in England.

Grace stood in the narrow hallway and looked around while taking off the silky scarf from her neck.

"Thank you, James. What a wonderful house."

"It was a bachelor's house in the past, so please ignore a few things. I will arrange to make it more comfortable for you."

The spacious room in the middle of the house grabbed all her attention. It seemed to be the main sitting room. A wellpolished piano dominated the space and Grace couldn't hide her emotions when she saw it, but stopped herself from running to it. In her mind she already imagined herself playing the piano every day.

"I see what your eyes are on." James gave her a genuine smile. She was thrilled to see him smiling and thought that maybe there was hope, that he loved her.

"I didn't expect to see a piano, and I appreciate it."

"It has been there for ages, but nobody was allowed to play. I keep it in memory of my mama." James stopped in the middle of the room, staring at the piano. Then, moving his gaze towards Grace, he probably read the silent question on her face.

"You can play, darling, it's all right. Only *you*! But please not when I am at home."

She decided not to ask why. James's expression suddenly changed. Possibly hearing piano music still hurt, as it reminded him of his mother. He rushed out of the room and pointed to the right wing of the house saying that it was hers. He then, abruptly, disappeared into the left wing, shouting, "The servants will show you around. You can make a few changes, but not in my part of the house!"

What did that mean, not in *his* part of the house? *Not now*, she said to herself, *ask him later*. Grace turned her attention back to the sitting room, which had big bay windows on three sides walls. Their fully open shutters were letting the light in. The French doors led to a long wooden verandah, covered with greenery growing down from the roof. Grace observed the manicured lawn, a tennis court, and flowering shrubs and trees beyond the verandah. Her eyes caught sight of a picture on the wall. It was of James in his khaki military uniform. As an officer he also wore a Sam Browne belt. It sat on him perfectly. The only item which frightened her was the revolver attached to his belt.

"Memsahib, you are probably tired after such a long journey. Would you like to sit down and have a lemonade, or tea?"

Grace was indeed. Her relief over arriving in Bombay and finally getting off the ship had been short-lived. The next day she had to get on a plane, as James had managed to arrange for them to fly from Bombay to Calcutta on a Dakota transport aircraft. Grace had never flown before in her life. She was terrified and exhausted after that.

"Oh, yes please, Zia. A glass of lemonade would be lovely." Zia quickly glided out of the room; her feet didn't make a sound.

Grace eyed a large armchair in the corner of the verandah and slowly sank into the soft seat. Closing her eyes, she was thankful that, finally, this long, terrifying journey had come to an end.

The calm atmosphere and the friendliness of her new maid made Grace feel relaxed. After a short nap, she freshened up and continued to explore the house with Zia's help, who also introduced her to the other servants. There were four male servants: the driver; the man who helped them with their luggage, who was James's batman; and a houseboy, who would serve James and Grace at the table during meals. The fourth boy was a punkah wallah, who manually operated the fan to cool the air in the house. There were two female servants: Zia, whom Grace already knew, and the cook, who was an old Indian woman who rarely spoke to anyone, but cooked delicious meals according to Zia. She explained how important it was to have a cook who could prepare not only Indian dishes, but European and British ones too. Zia promised Grace that she would take care of every dish for memsahib.

The house was clean and well prepared, particularly the room intended for Grace. She was surprised that a separate room had been arranged for her but didn't ask why. The room was lovely and bright. Next to the bed stood an old Victorian wardrobe with a fulllength mirror on its left-hand door. There was a cream-coloured fabric armchair near the window, next to the small table in the corner. Grace remembered that the house had not been fully prepared for her arrival, so she dismissed the lack of other furniture or ornaments in her room. Everything was new to her, the country, the food, the people and their language. She had expected James to explain what was important and to be there to answer her questions, but he was gone and it left her confused.

That evening, when she came to dinner, she found her husband still hadn't returned. The only person she could find was Zia, waiting in the dining room. Grace looked at the pristine white linen covering the table.

"Zia, forgive me, but I don't know yet about the arrangements. Will my husband be back for dinner?" She slipped into her chair, glancing over at the empty seat at the top of the table.

"Memsahib, there is enough food if sahib comes back for dinner. He might not … because of work."

She was clearly trying to choose her words carefully. "I will set the table for two anyway." Zia was very sweet. It was obvious she was trying her best to make her mistress feel comfortable.

"It looks like I have been left on my own." Grace's dream of starting a new life together with her husband was crushed. His habit of disappearing hadn't changed, nor his chameleon mood.

As soon as Zia opened the lids of the buffet dishes, a sweet aroma of mixed spices enveloped the room. Her maid helped the houseboy, whose English was very poor, and explained what type of food was on the table. She kindly suggested that after a long journey, a light dish would be the best to start with. There was homemade chapatis, a dish made with potato and cauliflower called aloo gobi, cottage cheese, samosas made with vegetables, and rice with curry sauce. Also, mashed potatoes and chicken stew were placed on the table just in case Grace preferred something she was used to, as well as a big piece of meat for James. Zia mentioned a dish called kedgeree, in case Grace wanted fish. For dessert there was rice pudding served on banana leaves. Zia explained that most Indian food was spicy and it usually took time for British people to get used to it. Grace thanked Zia for such careful consideration in preparing her first meal at her new home.

Grace barely touched her dinner. She was not as hungry as she thought, but in gratitude to the cook, she tried some of the food. She did enjoy the rice pudding though.

As she was leaving the room, she said, "Zia, please make sure all the servants of the house are fed."

With wide eyes Zia replied, "But memsahib, we can't touch the food from your table!"

"Nonsense. Of course, you can and you must. Don't tell me that you would throw away all of this. I barely touched it."

"But sahib ..."

"*Sahib* is not here. Please don't worry about him."

"Bless you, memsahib, bless you," whispered Zia a few times.

That first day in her new home, Grace felt lonely not only at the dinner table, but in bed too. James didn't come back that night.

A new life in India

Meeting the Raj

James came back home the next morning and was at breakfast as if nothing had happened. When Grace entered the room, he was already sitting at the top of the oval table.

While tearing a chapati apart, he said, "Morning, darling. Hope you slept well."

"Morning, James." She glanced over the table, gave her husband a kiss on the cheek and chose to sit on his right.

"We are invited for dinner tomorrow at eight o'clock." He dipped a piece of chapati into a small bowl of homemade cheese and then put it straight into his mouth.

"That's lovely." Grace held a teacup in her hand, while she watched her husband eating. She was still feeling tired but decided not to object to the invitation. "Where is this?"

"Major Spencer, his wife, Margaret, and their daughter, Hannah, are our neighbours. They kindly invited us over. I have known them for years. It's important for you to make a few friends, but not *too* many. I am sure Margaret will answer all your questions. Also, I was promoted to the rank of captain before I left to go to England. So, there will be some celebration."

"Ah, James, I didn't know that. Congratulations! I am really happy for you. Good news to start."

"Thank you, darling. Please be ready in time. Margaret is very particular about punctuality. As the wife of an officer, you must learn these things."

"I will be ready whenever you need me to be ready." She took a sip of her tea and asked, "I need to know when you will be at home so that I can make arrangements for dinners or breakfasts."

"There is no need for you to do anything for me. My schedule is quite erratic, but for yourself … the servants are at your disposal. They know everything about the house." He pointed at the houseboy in the corner of the room.

"Don't I need to know when you are at home?"

James gave her a strange look and stopped eating. He grinned. Then he finished his coffee before he answered.

"Grace, you will get to know my schedule in time. Please don't worry about anything. I guess you will be busy with the house for the next few weeks. Margaret knows everyone and can recommend furniture shops for you and where to buy the best linen, silk and whatever you need." He got up and Grace gasped, covering her mouth with her hand. James was wearing shorts—it was not his everyday uniform that shocked her but the weapon attached to the side of his belt.

James kissed her on the cheek. "Get used to it. Have you already forgotten who you are married to?" He was on the way out when he added, "See you soon," leaving Grace with her thoughts.

The exterior of the Spencers' house was exactly the same as their house. It was two hundred metres away, within the Raj community. When they walked in, Grace was promptly introduced to the Spencer family. Major Spencer was in his late fifties, clean shaven and a wellmannered gentleman. He took a step towards her and put out his hand.

"Brian," he introduced himself. An aroma of sandalwood touched her nose.

"Lovely to meet you, Brian." She paused for a second. "Grace."

"Welcome home, Grace, to India. Welcome home."

"Good evening, sir," said James before she could even thank Brian.

"Ah, Clifford, we finally get to see you settle down. Congratulations to both of you!" He patted James on his shoulder.

"Grace, how are you finding India?"

"Oh, I'm getting used to the heat and humidity."

"The heat, oh yes. In this country, the punkah wallahs are always guaranteed work. Right, James?"

When Margaret approached them, Brian apologised to Grace and took James to another room to discuss some business. Margaret had a big smile on her face when she greeted Grace. After introducing herself, she took Grace's hands in hers and showed her around their house. The warm welcome and cheerful atmosphere made Grace feel comfortable. Their daughter, Hannah, was a pretty, seven-year-old girl with curly brown hair. She gave Grace a big, sincere smile then hid her eyes behind the doll she was holding. It was obvious that she was very happy to see a new guest. Her mother then asked Hannah to play on the verandah and be quiet.

"James told me that you are from Ireland," Grace said to Margaret, while smiling at Hannah who had run away from them.

"Yes, I am from Belfast. Brian is from England, Essex. We have lived here for so long that I sometimes forget about my life back in Ireland. Hannah was born here."

Grace looked at Hannah who had joined a local girl on the verandah. Next to them was a boy, the punkah wallah.

Margaret caught her glance and answered Grace's unasked question. "She is Hannah's nanny. They call them ayahs here."

"Ayahs? The girl looks very young. How old is she?"

"She is only twenty years old, but she is good. We have gone through some difficulties to find a good ayah. We even tried a Christian one from Goa. She was much older and more experienced, but that did not work out. The Indians may be lazy, but at least in the end they do what you want them to. At a young age they learn quickly and are more flexible. The only problem is their English is very poor or nonexistent."

"My maid, Zia, speaks quite good English. I was impressed actually."

"Oh, lucky you. I hope you will be fortunate with your ayah as well when you have children."

Grace hadn't thought about children yet and felt awkward. She hadn't even had a chance to discuss it with James. It was a sensitive topic for her to talk about. Margaret saved the situation by changing the subject.

"And where are you from in England?" Margaret asked.

"From the south, but I was born in Ireland, Donegal."

"Really? Join the club!"

"Unfortunately, I don't remember my parents. I was only two years old when they died and was raised by my grandmother in England."

"Oh, dear, so sorry to hear that. Losing your parents at that age ..." Margaret didn't finish as her husband walked into the room with James. Then their housemaid informed them that dinner was ready.

Grace saw James relaxed for the first time. When he spoke with Brian, he smiled a lot, which was rare. They shared jokes between them and spoke of their love of whiskey. Grace was puzzled and wondered what had happened to James she knew. She observed him carefully from time to time during dinner. It seemed that James was in his element with Brian. Most of their talk was about their duties and the political situation in India and England. Sometimes they lowered their voices to say something and would have a cheeky smile on their faces afterwards. She had never seen her husband this way. It was clear he enjoyed Brian's company. James's dominant character actually seemed comfortable with someone of a higher military rank than him. Brian was also older than James. Grace compared him to Lord Clifford and wondered why James couldn't be the same with his father or with her.

Her eye caught his smile and she felt her heart rate increase. She loved him in that moment. She wanted him to be like this all the time, with that smile on his face. His eyes were smiling too and she felt the desire to rush to him and be surrounded by his happy aura and preserve the moment forever. She forgot about him being obnoxious. What had changed him and why? *I must try to understand my husband*, Grace said to herself, *and try to find the way to his heart.* Maybe she could give him the love he was looking for and he would love her back.

During dinner, Margaret told Grace that Brian had the rank of major in the British Army and explained what that meant. He had taken James under his wing a few years ago and had helped with his recent promotion from second lieutenant to captain. She added that it would be best for Grace not to ask her husband too many questions about his job, saying their husbands had a lot of duties and wanted to come home to rest, not to be questioned. Then Margaret changed the subject again. Grace noticed that she was quite skilled at switching from one topic to another.

"I assume you have not yet met anybody here?"

"No, we just arrived two days ago."

"Not to worry, my dear, you will have plenty of time. Unfortunately, you have arrived at a very turbulent time. You probably picked up on that on your way here."

"Yes, I did," said Grace in a lowered voice, remembering the children with hands stretched out towards their car on their way to the house. "Is there anything that can be done to help those people, especially poor children? I saw so many of them begging for food on the streets and was shocked. I didn't know that it was so bad here." Grace looked at the table full of food.

"Honestly, darling," Margaret said to her. "Absolutely nothing more can be done for them." She touched Grace's chin lightly. "Such is life out here. We do as much as we can."

"I would like to help them."

"Ah, that is very sweet of you, my dear, but there are the rules of the time and place to consider. And who can do what. You have just set foot off the ship and are already impatient.

Take your time. There is a lot for you to learn, including how to help the less fortunate. Just remember, they have a caste system and your help might work against them." Before Grace even had a chance to react, Margaret continued, "Also, I would advise you to be careful with your servants."

"Why? I found them all nice."

"They have a reputation … how to say it without frightening you? They make you feel alert all the time. Watch them. Try not to get too friendly with them anyway." She glanced at her husband. "Our position here, my dear, is to preserve and uphold the British Empire, and support our husbands. Do not forget, we are officers' wives. You have to think of our husbands' reputations, and yours as well."

"My maid Zia seems like a lovely girl." Grace ignored Margaret's comment about the British Empire, to which she was indifferent.

"Zia … hmm. You have just arrived and are already fond of your maid. Oh, dear. Do not let their friendly faces fool you."

"Margaret, did you have a bad experience with your servants?"

"Apart from the experience with ayahs? Let me think … most of the servants are painfully slow. You have to keep them on their toes. What else? Ah, it is not easy to find a good cook."

Grace wanted to say that she knew that, because Zia told her so, but decided not to mention her maid again.

"They also steal food; would you believe it? Whatever you do for them, whether you treat them well or offer them food, they will still pilfer. Unbelievable. I gave up after a while." She threw her hands up.

"But, Margaret, they're starving on the streets."

"We cannot feed them all, you know. Some of us are victims of other people's decisions." She added straight after, "And there are so many damn snakes here." As she said this, Margaret looked at Hannah, probably to make sure she hadn't been in the garden where snakes frequently lurked.

"Margaret, sweetheart, please do not scare Grace with your stories," intervened Brian. "It is true about snakes, but the servants know what to do. The best deterrent was, of course, our mongoose, Josephine. Until Margaret packed her off." He looked at James and winked.

"Oh, no, please do not remind me about that favourite pet of yours. It was sneaking around all the time and when there were no snakes about, it was stealing food from the kitchen. Dreadful looking animal, dreadful," Margaret replied in disgust.

"I know you did not like her, Margaret, but she did the job. We never had snakes in the house or garden while she was here. Grace might consider getting one. If you change your mind, let me know. I can …"

"Brian!" said Margaret in her firm voice. "Please do not annoy me. Just the thought of having that creature in our house again makes me sick. Stop it!"

Brian laughed. “Very well, my darling, very well.” He turned back to James and they continued their conversation. Margaret shook her head and rolled her eyes.

“Mongoose? Josephine?” Grace had never heard of this animal. She covered her grin with her hand.

“I know. I know. Brian always gives animals funny names.” Seeing Grace trying to hide her smile, Margaret said, “Unfortunately, that name could not disguise the look of the beast.”

“I have yet to see a mongoose.”

“Of course, it is up to you, my dear, but I would not recommend it. Why do you need an ugly-looking animal in the house? Especially when children are around. There are other ways to prevent snakes coming inside.” She pointed at her ayah. “She is actually quite good at flushing them out. She caught one the other day with her hands – I could not believe it.”

“Oh, no! Really?”

“Your face, Grace!” Margaret laughed. “Do not worry, you will get used to it soon. Most of the snakes are harmless, but watch out for the cobras. And the monkeys! They are everywhere.” She took a dish from the table and passed it to Grace.

“Try this. It is not spicy at all. The only Indian dish I can tolerate.”

"What is it? Smells good."

"This is called korma. They cook chicken in a lot of coconut milk. It is rich and creamy, but not as spicy as other Indian dishes."

Grace tried it and said, "That's quite tasty, I like it. Mild enough."

"I am glad you like it, my dear. You will survive here then."

Grace could tell that Margaret missed Ireland because, for the rest of the evening, she talked only about her home town. They sat on the verandah in the fading light of an Indian sunset while their husbands went out into the gardens for a smoke.

The conversation ended with Margaret asking, "What about tea next week at my house? I am sure you are already missing the tradition of afternoon tea and scones. My lemon drizzle cake is fabulous, loved by many."

"That would be lovely, thank you very much, Margaret. I love tea. And I would love to try your famous lemon cake!"

"You are in the right place for tea, my dear. I miss the company of a young intelligent lady. There is a lot I have to tell you about life in India. Also, we have a Ladies' club here. So, they are all eager to meet you. Take your time to settle down, then get ready for many tea parties." She smiled and gave Grace a warm look, like her nana used to.

Marriage struggles

Crushed dreams

In September of 1944, Grace was sitting on her verandah, gazing at the rhododendrons in the garden. The punkah wallah was busily keeping her cool. She was experiencing confusing thoughts about her marriage. She didn't understand her husband's changeable behaviour. Was it because of his military duty or because of her? She might be able to understand her husband if only he would share his feelings, but since their first intimate night, James had never shown her the same tenderness and love.

"There you are. Good afternoon my dear." Margaret walked onto the verandah. "The door was open and nobody was around. Where is Zia?"

Grace got up to greet her friend. "Good afternoon, Margaret. How are you? She is visiting her family and will be back soon. Would you like some lemonade, or would you prefer tea?"

"Lemonade is fine, thank you dear. It seems that you are caught up in your own world. We have not seen you for a while in the Ladies Club." Margaret gave Grace a soft smile and sat on the chair next to her. "Everyone is asking about you there."

"That's very nice of them."

"How long has it been, a year since you came to India?"

"Yes, about a year. It seems like it has all happened in one day."

"I do not want to be rude or nosey, but is there something bothering you my dear? I can tell, you are a bit sad and have been quiet for weeks. If somebody from the community said something to upset you, please let me know. There are some women here wearing the most expensive handmade hats, but you know, those hats are only covering empty spaces."

Grace couldn't hide her smile and felt supported. "I am all right Margaret, thank you. I was lucky enough not to meet such women." She didn't know what to say further. She couldn't find any interest in attending numerous parties where the main activity was gossiping about others or their love affairs. Her mind was occupied with how to make her marriage work. She didn't mean to avoid meeting Margaret. "All is well. It's just …"

Grace struggled with words. She looked over to the photo in the silver frame which was on table next to her. The photo was of her and James on their wedding day. Before she could continue, Margaret asked, "Are you missing your husband?"

"I am…I understand that he has a job and it can be demanding."

"Oh, yes, it is very demanding, but you do not need to worry about it. I remember when James was a bachelor, he was miserable and now he has you. I think the two of you are a good match and can make a lovely family. Just think about it. Think about a family."

Grace knew what Margaret was talking about. She meant children.

"The power is always in a woman's hands. You are the queen in your own house. Do not worry what is going on outside. There are too many upsetting things and events. Focus on your family. Our job as wives is to make our husbands happy. But first, we must make ourselves happy, don't you think so?"

"You are always right, Margaret." Grace looked at her friend gratefully and filled up their empty glasses with more lemonade.

When Margaret left, Grace was thinking about what she said about family and the power in women's hands. Grace would argue with that. It was James who held the power over her and controlled everything in her life. She couldn't say that to Margaret. She found it difficult to accept that her marriage wasn't as happy as she first imagined. James was aggressive and distant, often coming home drunk and, for some reason, angry with her. She tried to talk to him, but that made him even more angry. How could she make it work and start a family? In her first year in India, Grace learned enough about the lives of British Army officers and blamed the military service for what it had done to her husband. She continued to justify her husband's behaviour until one fateful day.

James had, once again, come back drunk. He was still in his military uniform and, although he had already had enough, he went to pour more of his favourite whiskey. He glowered angrily at her, then asked her to sit next to him on the verandah.

"I heard you have become a party girl," he barked, with his gaze dancing over the surface of the whiskey.

"Party girl? I don't think so. I just joined Margaret a few times at the Ladies' club. You told me to make friends." She gave him a weak smile.

"Ladies' club … huh." He rubbed the back of his head.

Grace tried to work out the shade of her husband's mood. Every fibre of her body began to tingle. The intense smell of whiskey and tobacco so close to her started to irritate her nose.

"How often?"

"How often what?"

"How often are you at the club?"

"James, I don't know what this is about, but I can assure you that I'm not really interested in going there often. I only go on some occasions when it would be rude not to."

"You are too young to understand. I just want to warn you

that there is a lot of gossip which you don't need to hear. It could be as infectious as Indian mosquitos."

"Don't worry, I am vaccinated from that."

James chuckled under his breath. "Huh … she is vaccinated. Are you trying to be smart now?" He suddenly stretched out his hand and grabbed her chin, moving her towards him. Grace bit her tongue. This proved once again that she couldn't speak freely with her husband. Anything she said he could turn against her.

"James …" she said, her voice lost in her throat. But something made him drop his hand and Grace was able to pull back. He took a long sip of his whiskey.

"Did you hear me or not? Less contact with that brood …" He stopped, dusting off his trousers. "And … please stop playing Florence Nightingale. Keep your mind out of that business. My job is hard enough putting food on our table and buying you whatever you need."

"What is the harm in giving the children some food?"

"It's fine as long as it's not bought using my bank account."

"James, I have my own money."

"Your own money? I thought you were smarter. It's our money! I am surprised that you haven't got it yet. Do you know how stressful my job is? Plus, I have to manage our family affairs in England. Your only role is to be my dutiful wife. That's it. So, do that one damn thing right!"

"James, you are barely home. What do you expect me to do?"

"Barely home? I am serving king and country! And you … you still find a reason to complain. It seems you fail to grasp the nature of our circumstances here. It falls to me, then, to show you," he shouted, standing up. Grace immediately regretted her words and realised that she might have provoked her husband. His jaw was like a rock and his eyes full of anger.

In a fleeting second, James grabbed her wrist and pulled Grace off her seat. He didn't take his hand off her until they were in his bedroom. The door slammed loudly behind them, and she felt her stomach twist. When he let her hand loose, she stepped away from him.

"You have me now and all my attention." He took off his military jacket and dropped it on the floor. "I don't think you can find a reason to complain now. I am all *yours*." And with that he threw her onto his bed.

"James, what are you doing? Please …" Grace put both her hands against his chest.

"Too late for that question. You have to be reminded about your duty and you asked for this." There was mockery in his voice.

Grace held her breath while he took off his clothes. James hauled her dress up to her neck, putting one of his hands on her jaw and squeezing it hard. He forced himself upon her. It was an awful experience and shocked her to her bones. It was one thing to tolerate his lack of tender feelings, but another to endure his abuse. She was deeply hurt.

In the morning, Grace was in pain. The ordeal had brought back memories of their wedding night when he had shown his aggression in bed for the first time. It made no sense how much he had changed towards her since they had married. All that morning she cried in the bathroom. She couldn't even look at herself in the mirror. She wanted to go home, back to England.

When, a month later, James came home drunk again, Grace locked herself in her bedroom. He almost broke down the door trying to open it, scaring all the servants with his shouting. There was a moment of silence. Then came a sudden roar, followed by the sound of something heavy falling to the floor.

"Memsahib, memsahib." It was Zia's voice. "Sahib has fallen and he is bleeding."

Grace opened the door and followed Zia towards the moans coming from another room. There she found James, lying on the floor, his hand covered in blood. Next to him was a broken whiskey glass. It was with some difficulty that the two of them managed to drag him onto the sofa. As Grace began tending to his wound, Zia left the room silently.

"I love you … Don't leave me," he slurred.

He sounded delirious and his eyes were closed. Nevertheless, Grace froze. Never before had he spoken such words of love to her. Usually, he was so withdrawn and clumsy when it came to expressing his feelings, beyond the odd compliment, or moment of gentleness, or a suddenly bewitching voice. But that was all before their wedding. Grace looked at her husband and waited for him to say something else.

"Mama. Ma-ma, where are you?"

So, the delirious words of love were for his mother, and not his wife. Grace continued to tend to the wound on his hand, but then James jerked it back and waved it out of the way.

"I hate him! I'm going to kill him!"

Grace took both of her husband's hands and gently pressed them against his chest. She watched him as he turned his head from side to side.

"She looks like you," he continued. "Please stay. I need you!"

For the first time, Grace registered pain on her husband's face. She felt sorry for him. James had never before fully opened up to her. There was so much hurt inside him that he was writhing all over. She forgot about her resentment towards him, about the fact that he had hurt her. All she thought about now was how to ease James's suffering, as he spoke, comparing her to his mother, about love. He might be delirious, but she had no doubt that, here before her, for the first time, lay the real James, a man who had been traumatised as a child by the loss of his mother and the lack of love from his father. No one had ever loved him as much as his mother. All this time he just wanted to be loved, with all his flaws, and free of judgement. Grace didn't notice she was crying until a tear fell on her hand.

"Don't leave me. Don't go, don't go!"

"I'm here, James," she said. "I'm not leaving."

Grace kissed her husband on the cheek. Soon afterwards, he fell asleep. By the time he woke, the whole night had passed and most of the next day too.

"What happened?" He was looking at his hand while still lying on the sofa.

"You fell," she said, coming to sit beside him.

"I don't remember anything."

"Don't worry. Your hand is fine. Just a small wound."

"Thanks," he said, his voice subdued, "for looking after me."

Grace put her hand on his shoulder and James covered it with his hand. "I'm your wife, James." She wanted to say that she loved him, but she couldn't. Grace wanted him to tell her that he loved her, but that was not coming. She leaned over and kissed him on the cheek.

Grace was able to believe that they had finally found their feet as a couple, and they resumed a normal married life. James began returning home more often. He was sometimes not in the mood, but she could see he was trying his hardest to control himself when he was around her. She, in turn, reminded herself that military service left its mark.

Once, in November of 1944, James disappeared for a long while. Worried, Grace asked Margaret if she knew anything. Margaret replied that Brian was stationed elsewhere and couldn't tell her anything about James. Then Grace began to notice sidelong glances directed at her when she and Margaret attended various events. The gossip about her husband began to reach her. If in England, it hadn't been obvious to anyone, here James's alcohol addiction and love affairs didn't go unnoticed. She learned from Margaret that it was the Raj lifestyle in India and it was common behaviour, particularly among those in highranking positions. Grace couldn't believe that Margaret was telling her this without expressing any concern for herself. She hesitated to ask further questions. She didn't want to know anything more than she had already found out. If it was the truth, she was embarrassed by her husband's behaviour, but still had hope for them both.

A month after that conversation, Grace was sitting alone in the drawing room, reading a novel, when she heard the sound of James's car coming, fast, up the driveway. Through the window, she saw that he was in the driver's seat. It wasn't long before the house door sprang open and then he was there, standing in front of her, his uniform filthy and his face full of anger as he stared at her. She was about to say something – she didn't know what – but before she could, he left, slamming the door behind him. All that week, he drank, and it wasn't difficult for her to avoid him altogether. Then, the day of the annual Christmas Ball, which was usually held in mid-December, he surprised her by turning up downstairs in his tails.

"Oh ..." Grace hadn't expected her husband wanting to go out, as the day before he had been sick with a very bad hangover. She missed the Christmas Ball the previous year when they arrived in India because she came down with a heavy flu and she hoped that they would stay home this year as well.

"I see you are not ready. Did you forget what the day is today?"

"I thought we were not going. Sorry."

He looked sober or at least as close to sober as James got.

"You still have time. I will pop in to see Major Spencer and then come back for you." He checked his watch and moved the leather strap around his wrist, making sure it was still a good fit. "And then we are off. I have to meet someone there. It's important. So, hurry up."

They arrived together at the Grand Hotel in Calcutta, arms linked, as befitting a loving couple. As they walked through the crowded room, many people greeted them. Grace smiled sweetly at everyone. The hotel's huge ballroom was beautifully decorated. She had never seen such luxury in England. The Raj behaved as if there was no war and as if there was no poverty outside the walls of the hotel. People were cheerful and happy, dancing and flirting. The tables were piled high with food and drinks. It was certainly the most lavish feast of the year.

The room had many statues, decorative gold detailing and beautiful drapes that fell from the ceiling to the floor. Sparkling garlands and colourful dresses were everywhere, and big golden peacock tails hung on each wall of the room. Grace started to feel a bit dizzy. She had never been so relieved as when she suddenly spotted her friend Margaret among the guests.

"Your husband will no doubt want to enjoy the company of the other men, to discuss whatever dull things that have them so fascinated," said Margaret when they approached her.

"I suppose she will be safe with you, Margaret."

"Indeed, she will. Off with you." Margaret smiled.

"Right you are." Before he left, he put his lips to Grace's ear. "I will be back for you soon."

Margaret showed Grace around and told her that the Christmas Ball had been held in this hotel for years. It was a huge annual event. Whatever disaster might be erupting outside the walls, the ball would go on.

"I find that shocking," said Grace.

"Indeed, it is, dear, but it is outside our control."

"Is there any charitable organisation in Calcutta? I would like to be involved and help people, especially those poor wretched children."

"All of us, the wives I mean, take any opportunity we can to help children. I will give you more information about the Red Cross later. For now, let's enjoy the evening. Please try not to worry about anything, my dear."

Grace promised that she would do her best before asking for directions to the ladies' room. When she came back, she couldn't find Margaret. It was difficult to breathe in such a large, crowded hall and she didn't know anybody so decided to go upstairs. Margaret had told her that up there were a few meeting rooms, bedrooms, a restaurant and another ladies' room if the one downstairs was busy. Anyway, it was a good time to explore the hotel and avoid encountering people on her own.

She passed the restaurant full of people. Gosh, they were everywhere. People, food, drinks, but at least upstairs the music was not so loud. Grace walked along the corridor, looking at the paintings. She wasn't paying attention, turning left and then right, and ended up in what was probably one of the hotel wings. While standing there calculating which way to go back, she overheard some voices not far away. Grace slowly started to move in the direction of the sounds, which turned into an incomprehensible moan. One of the room doors was slightly open.

Grace was embarrassed to look and began to leave, when a female voice said, "Why did you stop? We don't have much time today and you know the way I like it, so, hurry up, *my sahib*." The woman said it playfully. Then, breathing loudly, she continued in a teasing tone, "By the way, I have prepared a surprise for you, but not now. If you are a good boy, you will get it later."

My sahib? Grace might have supposed that one of guests was hiding there with a hotel maid, but the woman spoke in a perfect English accent. She was definitely from the Raj. The sounds of a zipper being pulled down and sighs of arousal then followed. Grace could feel her face was on fire. The two people behind this door were lovers. It was a sexual act by the sound of it. She turned to leave as quickly as possible, but before she figured out the way to run, she recognised the voice of the man in the room.

"Oh, you like to tease me. Come on, get closer, my sweet pussy. I will give you what you are asking for."

Pussy? Her brain refused to process that word. But it wasn't the vulgarity that was so insulting, but who said it and in what tone. *James!* By the time an earsplitting slap on the woman's body and a loud laugh reached her, Grace was already at the end of the corridor. She rushed down the stairs and stood, rooted to the spot, in the same place she had been before. *What had just happened?* It was one thing to hear gossip about her husband's love affairs and another to witness one of them for herself. She looked down at the floor and tried to slow her breath. When she had managed, she glanced over the people's heads searching for Margaret. Two women from the club waved at her from across the room. She waved back but kept standing where she was. Before she could process her thoughts further, a man approached her.

"What a fabulous event, isn't it? You seem a bit lost. Is this your first time here? By the way, I am John Gore." He threw his hand out to her.

"Grace Clifford." She let him touch her hand briefly and pulled it back, pretending she was straightening her dress. He pressed a handkerchief to his forehead.

"How do you ladies stay so fresh in such unbearable heat?"

She didn't reply, looking at her feet.

"Grace, would you like something to drink or maybe a dance?"

"No, thank you. I am fine." Her body stiffened and her eyes kept searching for Margaret in the crowd of dancing people.

"Come on, it will cheer you up. Let's dance. I can amuse you." When John staggered closer, a strong smell of alcohol reached her nose. He touched her hand. Grace stepped back and moved her hand away from him. He lurched towards her, grabbed her hand again and held it tightly. Grace struggled. She didn't know what to do.

"All right, I will go with you. Just please let go of my hand."

John released Grace's hand, but stood next to her, staring at her. All she could think about and hope for was that James wouldn't see her with this drunk man. Grace politely conversed with the rude man to take his thoughts of dancing with her away, but she couldn't help looking around the room nervously. Sure enough, after five minutes, she saw James blustering his way towards her, his face thick with anger.

"I was … waiting for Margaret," she stammered at him, as the drunk man peeled away.

James took her rigid hand and walked across the room, keeping Grace beside him, to get a glass of wine. He didn't get one for her. For the rest of the evening, he never took his eyes off her. He spoke to other people, but not to her. She felt guilty for some reason, like it had been her there, upstairs, not him.

They left the event early, without even telling Margaret, and returned home together. Grace said little on the way back. She watched her husband's every move in fear. He was drunk, as always. There was no sign of the servants when they entered the house. In her bedroom, Grace hadn't even taken off her evening dress when James entered without knocking. He pulled off his tie and began to undo the buttons on his shirt. Then he stopped, came closer to Grace from behind and started kissing her on the back of her neck.

"You looked beautiful in this black dress today, darling. Just cover your shoulders next time. They are only for me to see. You have such fair skin," James said in the same languid voice he had used that night in the gate lodge. He began running his hands up and down her back. The tone and language he had used with that other woman was different. It stuck in her mind. The smell of alcohol from him overpowered her perfume. Lifting her hair, he tried to find the clasp of her dress with his other hand, then cursed loudly before tugging angrily at it until she heard the sound of fabric tearing.

What followed next shocked her. James threw her roughly onto the bed and began to rip off the rest of her clothes. When she begged him to stop, he covered her mouth with his hand, continuing to greedily kiss her body. As though delirious again, he began muttering things that made no sense to her: how her beauty was ruining him; how she was to blame for everything; how she was a worthless wife, unable to give birth to a son; how she lived a carefree cheerful life, while her husband served his country.

Under the weight of his body, Grace gasped.

"Let me go. James, please let me go. I don't understand why you are making these accusations. I didn't do anything wrong. If you want children, please stop treating me like *this*." Her voice rose.

He slapped her across her face. A burning sensation immediately covered her cheek and neck. Her whole body shook. Tears filled her eyes. She kept her head still, the side that had been slapped turned upwards, not prepared to offer her other cheek to him. Grace could imagine her husband's hand a few hours ago *resting* on that woman's body, and now he was using the same hand to *hit* her, humiliating her. The blood in her veins heated. Another second and she would blurt out everything she wanted to say to him, but she refrained and lay there, motionless, with her eyes closed.

"Don't speak to me like that and don't scream! No one will come to your aid. In this house, everyone obeys me and only me! You can't even manage your servants."

When he finally rolled off her, Grace found she still couldn't move. For a while, all her attention was on the salty taste of blood on her lips. That, and the sound of him sniffling from his side of the bed. It was a while before she was able to take herself to the bathroom to clean up. She stayed there for a few minutes. Then she opened the door carefully to check if James was still in the room. Thankfully, he was gone. Grace breathed a sigh of relief and went straight to bed covering herself with a blanket and hiding her head under it.

In the morning, Grace decided to get up and go for breakfast. She didn't want James to come for her. Pain reverberated throughout her body, but she endured it. At least there were no bruises on her face, only a small bruise at the corner of her lips. Zia, she suspected, knew what had happened because all morning she was quiet and probably scared. All the servants were scared of James when he was angry. James was already at the table with the newspaper in his hands. They had breakfast in silence.

Afterwards, he glanced over at her. He noticed the bruise by her lips and leaned over to try to touch it.

Grace put her teacup down and slowly moved her head away.

"I didn't want that. Sorry."

Grace couldn't believe he had said *sorry*. She gritted her teeth and started to butter her toast. James opened up the newspaper again, probably because he wanted to cover his face. He was quiet for the rest of the morning. He was always quiet after *such* behaviour towards her. And though she was prepared, she knew a line had been crossed. A kind of tipping point. She could never trust her husband again. At that moment she just wanted to be left alone.

As though reading her mind, he spoke, "I'm leaving today and I won't be back for a couple of months. I can't tell you where I'm to be stationed, but I will send you a message if the opportunity arises. In the meantime, I would ask you not to go anywhere, including any events Margaret might invite you to."

"Is that a request or a command?"

He didn't answer her. He didn't need to. It was clear from his tone it was the latter. There was no need to tell her to stay at home while he was gone. She didn't want to go out by herself and face the social pressure of the Raj. It also became clear, in that moment, that Grace couldn't save her marriage. That she would never try to do so again. Her pride was deeply hurt. While she was in India, it would be impossible to leave him. She would have to endure James, but not his barbaric attitude towards her. Gathering her strength, Grace prepared to stand her ground. Her husband had just altered the way their lives would go. Upon returning home to England, hopefully soon, she would leave him. It meant divorce!

Angel

Spiritual growth

In the months that followed James's return, Grace rarely saw him. They spoke little to each other. If he was drunk, he went straight to his room. More often he simply didn't come home. This new distance between them was good for Grace. Despite her strong nostalgia for home, she found India an interesting country to learn about and explore. It was a damaged world with too much cruelty, disease and death, but still, somehow, within all of this, she could also sense a lot of compassion, love, bravery and ancient wisdom. *Who are these people?*

The more Grace learned about Indian people, the more she felt grounded. She even tried to cook Indian dishes. When she appeared in the kitchen for the first time all the servants gasped, but she didn't mind getting her hands dirty and always treated the servants with respect. She enjoyed this time in the house without her husband. Zia taught her how to wear a sari, and when Margaret visited her one day, she was shocked to see Grace in one. Grace didn't care; she could wear anything she wanted in her own house. Margaret was like her grandmother, sometimes sharp and sarcastic with her comments. She and Grace had a different point of view on many things but managed to keep a good relationship. Grace began painting again and spent much of her time with brushes in her hands.

"I'm always happy to order more supplies for you, memsahib, just let me know," Zia said to her once. "It pleases me to see you so happy when you are painting."

Grace was rediscovering herself. She began to meditate, and, through this, her mental well-being improved. Zia's former master introduced her to one of the best yoga and meditation tutors in Calcutta and, after just a few meetings, Grace was able to do it on her own. She loved it. Meditation didn't just help her to relax, she managed to take control of her thoughts and found that she could focus on what she wanted. Her imagination improved and her paintings became more artistic and colourful.

One day a suspicious sound in the bushes grabbed her attention. A local boy of about eight years old appeared in her garden. He was shy and huddled in a corner under a banana tree. When he stood up, she saw the bare skin on his malnourished belly was covered with dust and a torn, dirty piece of cloth draped around his bony hips. He had matted hair, partly covered with mud. Grace's heart shrank. When she took two steps towards him, the boy's almondshaped eyes were shot through with fear.

"Hello. Would you like to come out? Please don't be afraid." It seemed that her soft voice and the fact she had stopped moving towards him weren't helping; the boy only huddled further into his corner.

"Ah, it's him again!" said Zia, slowly approaching Grace from behind. "I have seen this boy before, memsahib."

"Have you? He is very skittish."

"Usually hiding in the same spot he is in now. I wanted to tell you, memsahib, but he was gone, until now."

"I haven't seen him before. What is his name?"

"I don't know. I understand that the boy is mute."

"Where does he live? What about his parents?"

"Looks like he is homeless. He is probably an orphan."

"Zia, please tell him that we want to give him food and maybe wash him. He looks pitiful." Tears welled in Grace's eyes. "Will he understand you?"

"I think so, memsahib."

"Bring him, please, into the kitchen and wash him with Dettol before he touches the food."

She watched Zia approach the boy, feeling certain he would bolt. To her surprise, after an initial hesitation, he followed her inside. In the kitchen, although he looked frightened, he obediently washed his hands when Zia directed him to do so. Then, quick as a flash, he grabbed a piece of bread from Zia's hands and ran away. It happened so fast Grace couldn't do or say anything to stop him.

A few days later he was back, and a couple of days after that too. Soon he grew bolder; he began to go into the kitchen for food and to get something to drink. Zia cleaned him up and taught him to nod in gratitude. His hearing was fine, and he seemed to understand what was said to him, though he never spoke. Luckily, he seemed to like it when Grace read books to him out loud. He liked the pictures and moved his finger along the pages.

Over time, this thin, darkeyed street boy got so used to Grace that he began to appear almost every day in her garden. He would sit on the ground for hours under a banana tree and watch Grace draw. He never tried to ask for anything, just sat quietly and waited to be called. He always nodded happily when Grace closed a book, indicating that the reading lesson was over for the day. A wide smile would spread across the boy's thin face, and his hands would form the shape of a pyramid, as if in prayer.

"You don't know it, but you have saved me from loneliness," she said to him once. "I think I will call you Angel. You must have been sent to me from above." Angel smiled, nodding his head.

One day, she drew his portrait. She and Zia laughed a lot when they showed it to him. He looked at himself with wide eyes. Then he took a step back and looked again, this time tilting his head. Coming closer, he pressed his nose against the canvas. Then he touched his painted face with his hand. It seemed like he had never looked in the mirror. The boy ran a hand through his hair, over his face, and turned to Grace, giggling out loud. He even sat down on the ground and grabbed his stomach. They all laughed.

"You understand that it is you?" asked Zia, pointing at the painting.

Angel nodded "yes". Then he formed his hands into a pyramid and gave Grace his fondest smile. She watched him while he ate a big piece of delicious lemon cake and washed it down with a mug of tea in delight. It felt precious to her to see at least one of those street children eating eagerly in her house. After stuffing his tiny belly with food, Angel ran up to Grace and gifted her with the most sincere and warm hug ever. She stood there with open arms, frozen in the air for a moment, before she gently placed them on the boy's head, ruffling his hair. He looked up at her with smiling eyes, stepped back and grabbed a pouch she had prepared with food for him to take away. Then he quickly ran to the end of the garden, where there was a small gap in the fence through which he could make his way out.

After that day, Angel disappeared. Whenever Zia was out for groceries, she looked for him on the streets, but to no avail. Grace was worried that something might have happened to him but Zia said that he had done this before, disappearing for days. Perhaps he would return one day. All Grace could do was wait and hope that her Angel would come back to her. The next few months passed as if they were only a few days. It was December of 1945. Soon, it would be time for the Christmas Ball again.

Tension began to return to Grace's body.

Crossroads of destiny

December 1945

Grace stood in the middle of the ballroom of the Grand Hotel feeling her heart sinking at having to be there again. She hadn't been out for months, and she certainly didn't want to go to an event where James would be watching her every move. She glanced briefly up the stairs, but fought the memory of that incident hard enough not to think about it. An intense aroma of cinnamon, cloves and fruit enveloped the room and reached her senses. The smell was coming from a bowl of hot punch on a large circular table, not far from her. She suddenly felt the urge to have some of that sweet, hot drink; it would give her an excuse to leave James's side. Her wish to escape had been fulfilled as Margaret approached them and managed to persuade James to let Grace go with her. Whatever Margaret said to him had James leaving without making a scene. Grace then saw Brian, who quickly said hello to her, before following James towards the bar.

Margaret had arranged for a few of Grace's paintings to be auctioned for charity that evening. Grace was glad to be able to help children in need. James didn't have much time for his wife and her new hobby. She suspected he had agreed to go to this annual event because he felt that he ought to appear with her in society from time to time; otherwise, everyone might think he was keeping her locked up in the house.

She had turned to him before they left and said, "As soon as the auction is over, I would like to go home."

"Good idea!" he replied with a grin on his face, but his tone was as firm as steel.

"Good idea," she echoed, looking down at her hands. At least he hadn't noticed yet that she wasn't wearing her wedding ring. She had taken it off a few days ago while she was painting. It had started to feel uncomfortable in the heat. Unfortunately, she hadn't been able to get it back on again. The swelling had not gone down enough, even though she had tried more than once. But deep down she was glad not to wear it.

Grace's paintings fetched more than she had hoped for, which made her very happy. When a servant circulated the room with drinks on a silver tray, Margaret took two glasses of champagne and passed one to Grace.

"Every painting bought. Well done!" she said. "Time to celebrate and where better to do it." She gestured at the beautiful ballroom with its chandeliers and high ceiling.

When Margaret then gently made it clear that James was busy with his own affairs and that Grace had nothing to worry about, Grace accepted it without question. The glass of champagne helped her relax a little. Margaret was then called in to finalise the auction papers, as she was one of the organisers of the event, but Grace didn't worry. However, while she waited for Margaret to come back, the noise and drunkenness around her seemed to intensify. It was almost painful to watch. So much food was left untouched, probably half of which would be thrown away after the ball, despite the fact that outside people were starving. After a while, Grace knew she needed fresh air. There was a huge terrace beyond the French doors, and as far as she could tell, there was no one on it. Not a single guest noticed as Grace, with glass of champagne in hand, made her way out there alone.

Outside, it was much darker, only the light from the high windows illuminated the middle of the terrace, while some glowing garlands hanging on a few potted palm trees adding spots of brightness elsewhere. Not wanting to be seen, Grace walked a little further into the shadows, where she stood, leaning against the stone railing around the terrace. While it was warm outside, it wasn't as stuffy as it was inside. For a while, Grace looked at the sky and took in its stars. She didn't notice she had been joined by a stranger until he spoke, and even then, he was just a shadow.

"The sky looks like a map of destinies, doesn't it?"

Grace turned towards the voice too quickly; her hand shook and she nearly dropped her glass. The young man was quickly at her side. With one hand he took the champagne from her, and with his other, he held her elbow with just his fingers so that Grace wouldn't fall. She wore a long sleeveless dress, and goosebumps immediately ran across her skin. Their eyes met in the same moment. She blamed her high heels for her unsteadiness. She hadn't worn them for so long and had forgotten how to stand in them. The stranger's citrus scent drifted through the air, reaching her nose. She took a deep breath, but then quickly came to her senses.

"Sorry, I didn't see you. I hope the champagne didn't get on your suit," said Grace as she tucked a strand of hair behind her ear. Her face filled with heat. She was glad it was dark.

"No need to apologise," he gave her back the glass of champagne. "It was my fault. I have a bad habit of turning into a shadow. I used to do this a lot as a child and scared everyone in the house. My father called me the invisible boy."

Grace and the stranger smiled at the same time. She ran her hand down her red silky evening gown, glancing away. Then they looked at each other again. She couldn't tell from his accent where the young man was from. His jetblack hair and his skin indicated he was Indian, but his skin colour was much lighter than other Indian people she knew. He stepped back a little and the light from the window passed over his face. Her gaze caught a glimpse of his grey eyes. He had exquisite facial features and was tall and muscular. He was dressed like a real gentleman and his English was perfect. She felt the warmth of his skin on her elbow when he touched her briefly.

"I'm Aadir," he said. "I have just returned from America and this is my first public event. I hardly know anyone here."

"Oh, this is not my first, but I hardly know anyone either." Grace was so intrigued by the stranger that she forgot to introduce herself. She continued, "From America? How interesting! Pardon my curiosity, Aadir, do you live in America?"

"I was born here in India. This is my home country, but I have lived in America for the last ten years. My father is from Calcutta. He needs my help with his business, so he asked me to come back."

"I see. It's very kind of you. I am sure your father is pleased to see you."

"Yes, he is. I think I've got into a trap. He won't let me leave his side again so easily." Aadir smiled widely. "What about you? How long have you been in India?"

"Just over two years."

"Two years? I guess that's enough time to get to know

India. Times are hard now here, like in many other countries, I suppose. But apart from that, do you like it here?"

"Yes … I do! Very much." Grace stuttered over her words. She felt confused, unsure of how to behave towards this man, yet unable to leave. She turned, clumsily, to place her glass on the top of the stone railing, and once again, Aadir managed to catch her in time.

"Oh, those heels!" Grace sighed and without thinking, she slipped her shoes off her feet. As she did so, Aadir held her hand so she wouldn't lose her balance, as though they had known each other for a long time. As they continued to chat, all her awkwardness fell away. She felt she could be herself with him, and wondered if maybe it was because they were both quite young. James, after all, was eighteen years older than Grace – forty-one to Grace's twenty-three. With him, she always felt like a little girl, whom he constantly controlled and dominated.

Aadir began to tell her about his country. After finding out what local dishes Grace had tried, he said that she hadn't yet experienced real Indian cuisine.

"Do you like seafood?"

"Seafood? Oh, yes, I do! I was born and raised by the sea. Any dish with fish or seafood is my favourite."

"Then you have to try macher jhol. It is Calcutta's traditional dish, spicy though, with garlic, ginger and turmeric. One of the best. The fish is marinated in turmeric, fried and then slowly cooked in tomato sauce with other spices. Add potatoes to it and yummy, a delicious dish! You should try it."

"I definitely will. Now, when you describe it in such detail, I feel hungry." Grace put her hand on her stomach.

"Allow me to tease you a little bit more." Aadir smiled slyly. "I would recommend you try two desserts, sandesh and mishti doi. The first one is made with milk or paneer and sugar, the second one with yoghurt."

"Stop. Stop! I couldn't eat today at all and now I feel like going inside and searching for all these dishes on that big table." They chuckled together.

They talked on and on, forgetting that there were two hundred people at the ball inside the hotel, even as the sounds of the music within played in the distance. Grace felt safe with Aadir, a feeling she had never had before. Somehow, she knew she could trust him, remembering how he held on to her, masterfully snatching the glass from her hands, and not letting her fall. How he gave her a hand when she took off her shoes. From somewhere, he brought a soft rug so that she wouldn't have to stand barefoot on the tiles of the terrace. She found herself watching his beautiful long fingers as he waved his hands around when he spoke. He told Grace about his busy life in America; that he had liked his life there and thought he would stay longer, but when he came back home to India, he realised how much he had missed his country. His story fascinated her. As he spoke, she couldn't really tell whether it was what he told her or the way he moved as he expressed himself that held her in his thrall. His eyes shone, his smile did too, and his voice had a calming effect. She was hypnotised by this handsome stranger.

"I probably talk a lot," he said.

She looked back at him, smiling. "No, not at all."

"Sorry, I just have not had such nice company for a long time. You know how to listen. I don't want to impose by asking you questions, but I would love to hear about you as well."

She was about to answer him, to tell him about White Cliffs and her grandmother, when she heard James's voice.

"Grace, are you there?"

Grace turned sharply. Her pulse pounded and she saw her fear reflected on Aadir's face.

"Is he calling *you*?"

"He is my husband. I have to go. Sorry." Grace grabbed her shoes and ran in the opposite direction.

Her last glimpse of Aadir was of him watching in dismay as she turned away and then ran into the shadows. From there, she watched as James approached him and called out to him by his name.

"Aadir. You have not seen my wife, have you?"

"James, I'm sorry, I haven't met your wife, only you. Has something happened?"

"No, it's all right. She just wanted to leave for home early, and our driver is waiting for her. I thought she was here. Good night then."

"Good night to you too."

After James had returned to the ballroom, Grace didn't dare go back to Aadir, but instead followed her husband at a safe distance. She soon managed to find Margaret, who told her what she had already heard – that the car was waiting for her outside the hotel.

"Margaret, will you tell James I'm going home? Please."

Before Margaret had a chance to reply, Grace ran off barefoot, shoes in her hand. Margaret would notice that, of course, but Grace didn't have time to explain anything. Luckily, James didn't return home that night, but still, she couldn't sleep. Tossing and turning all night, she couldn't understand why or how she had behaved the way she did. She had forgotten all about caution and had completely trusted this stranger. More than that, she hadn't been able to take her eyes off him.

What happened to me, she wondered. *Have I fallen in love? How could I fall in love with a stranger in just a few minutes?* She was still a married woman. She tried hard to forget Aadir, but her thoughts kept returning to the terrace. Grace smiled, embracing the pillow. Closing her eyes, she remembered the heat that came over her when Aadir touched her, how her skin had turned to goosebumps. This was the first time she had ever experienced such feelings. She had never felt like this with James. *Did I really love James? Why didn't I feel for him the way I felt for Aadir?* Someone she had only met once. Which was the real love? How was she to react to her new feelings?

Grace fell asleep with these questions in her head, hoping that the next day would give her answers.

Aadir

The sun after the storm

Waking early, Grace went into the garden and sat in her favourite spot, underneath the fig tree. So much had happened in the past few weeks since meeting Aadir at the Grand Hotel. Listening to the morning birdsong, she held a bunch of flowers. She relished the yellow hibiscus and white jasmine, as fresh as though they were still growing in the soil. Whenever James was away, a bouquet would arrive. Always without a note, but Grace never had to guess who they were from. These flowers always contained the colours orange or yellow, and it seemed to her there was a message in that – they symbolised the flame of love that burned between her and Aadir, the spark that gave them both hope. She had seen it in his eyes when they gazed at each other on the terrace, and she felt he had seen it in hers too.

It wasn't only flowers he sent. Aadir also gifted her with tea leaves that made the most delicious tea she had ever had, and sweets that she had never tasted before in her life. Everything was beautifully presented with a romantic touch. The last few weeks had changed Grace. She didn't feel lonely anymore. Her confidence grew stronger every day and she was ready to be braver.

Grace used to spend teatime with Margaret at the Grand Hotel. She now revived this tradition because she was eager to meet Aadir again. He had asked Grace twice already to meet him, sending a stealthy note through Zia. Grace later discovered that Zia used to work for his family. During Grace's first summer in India, she visited the Darjeeling tea plantation where the Cliffords' summer residence was and met the manager of the plantation, Kumar Gupta. He was responsible for running their tea production business and answered to Lord Clifford or to Oliver. What Grace didn't know then was that Kumar was Aadir's father. It was Kumar who had recommended Zia to James as a maid for his household. After she digested this information, she tried not to worry too much. She was happy to know that she could now trust Zia even more. Zia knew all about what Grace had to endure from James and probably hated him with all her heart. Grace wouldn't blame her if she did. Her and Zia's bond had grown much stronger.

The splendid flavour of black tea produced in Darjeeling was very popular in India, especially within the British Raj. Grace was looking forward to the afternoon tea ceremony with

Margaret in the Grand Hotel. She pulled out a mirror from her light green leather purse. Her dress, made from satin, was also green with white flowers embroidered on it. She smiled at her reflection in the mirror, seeing her emerald eyes and beautifully shaped eyebrows. Her long dark hair flowed down her back in waves with some resting on her shoulders. Grace moved a bit to see herself from behind in the mirror and remembered her grandmother saying that her straight back and long neck gave her natural elegance. She caught herself wondering if she was beautiful, which she hadn't done before. *Why is that?*

"What a striking beauty! May I join you, gorgeous lady? Sorry, I am a bit late. I guess you want to treat your slim figure with some of the delicious cakes they make here."

Grace stood up to give Margaret a light hug. "Hello, Margaret. You are very beautiful yourself. Is that the new dress you bought last week?"

"Yes, that is right. I eventually decided to follow your advice and be braver in wearing brighter colours. I think I look like a walking flower pot with these big pink bloom patterns on my dress. Is it too much?"

"Not at all, Margaret. You look younger in that dress. It sits well on you."

"Ah, my dear, thank you! Now, I feel better." Margaret smiled, suggesting, "Shall we start with a glass of champagne as usual? Despite living here for almost all my life, I am still struggling with this heat." She fanned her hand over her face.

"Why not? Champagne then," Grace cheerfully replied.

Later, they were holding teacups of the finest china in the middle of their tea ceremony when Aadir suddenly appeared from nowhere.

"Good afternoon, ladies. Mrs Spencer. Mrs Clifford."

Grace shivered, happily, her teacup frozen in the air.

"Good afternoon, young man." Margaret looked at Aadir intently. "Ah, I think I recognise you from the last Christmas Ball."

"Yes, Mrs Spencer, that was me, Aadir."

"Aadir. Yes, that's right, Aadir." She turned to Grace. "Grace, did you have a chance to meet Aadir that evening? I remember you left early."

"We met briefly, before I left." Grace blushed, trying to hide her eyes.

"Aadir, would you like to join us? If you are not in a rush." Margaret pointed with her eyes to the extra chair at the table. Grace was relieved that it was Margaret who asked Aadir to stay, not her. He accepted the offer with pleasure and thanked them both. "But please make sure to order extra cakes; I am not sharing."

They all laughed and felt at ease. In spite of the differences between them, Grace loved Margaret's sense of humour. If they didn't touch on the subject of the social lives of the

British wives in India, or talk of Grace helping Indians, she was comfortable around Margaret. Afternoon teas or shopping always helped to bring them closer.

"Brian said that you are very good at playing polo. Did you learn to play in India or in America?" It seemed Margaret was as keen to learn about Aadir as Grace was.

"In America. I was a member of the Hampton's Polo Club."

"Good for you. You are a very talented young man, Aadir. I knew it when I saw you." It was strange to hear something like that from Margaret, as if she were approving him for something. She continued to test him, "You lived there for a while. What did you do? Studying?"

"Yes, I did, Mrs Spencer. I've got a university degree and had a chance to work in a fivestar hotel in America. It was a good experience. I enjoyed it."

"That is very good. I like when people do not waste their time. I assume it will not be a problem for you to get a job in Calcutta, then? Many hotels here need to improve their services. Sorry for asking so many questions."

"Not at all. I'm ready to answer any question." He quickly glanced over at Grace with an almost invisible smile on his lips. "I'm not sure yet about a job in a hotel. My father needs my help at the moment on the tea plantations in Darjeeling."

"Tea plantations? Oh, yes." Margaret looked at her teacup. "You are coming to Darjeeling, then, this season? Your father is a very lucky man to have your help," she said in a lowered tone.

She then stopped talking for some reason and started to pay attention to her tea and desserts as the conversation moved on to the business of the plantations. Grace could read her friend's face. Margaret had a good memory. She had probably figured out that Grace left the ball that night with her shoes in her hand because she was running away from that brief meeting with Aadir. She gave Grace a cheeky sort of smile when she looked at her.

The waiter came to the table and passed the menu to Aadir. "Mrs Spencer, Mrs Clifford, if you don't mind, I will order a special tea blend for you," he said and started to ask the waiter about tea options.

Margaret turned her head to Grace and answered for both of them. "Of course, we do not mind. Grace and I love to try something new." Then she added, "Especially when the recommendation is coming from someone who has a better knowledge of teas than us." She gave Grace a wink.

"I can't wait to try. Thank you, Aadir." Finally, Grace found her voice.

Margaret and Grace complimented the new blend of tea that had a delicate flowery taste with a hint of some spice. After about an hour Aadir expressed his gratitude to them for having him to tea and left. Grace was upset that he couldn't stay for longer. She enjoyed his company very much.

Before she could say anything, Margaret started to speak. "What a good young man and very smart. He knew he could not be seen with us for too long and left just in time. I saw two ladies from our club arrived at the hotel. It would not be acceptable for him to be seen in our company."

"Why not? What's wrong with that?"

"Oh, my dear, you are still in that cloud of yours. I thought you would pick up and learn something about the rules and codes here for us."

"I did and I don't like them."

"I know. You stopped joining us at the club, but, Grace, it is essential to attend some events. Like it or not, you *must*. Your reputation is based on being there and who you are seen with in society. I only asked Aadir to join us because the Colonel took him under his wing, did you know that?"

"No. James does not discuss his work with me."

"I see. Look, Aadir is an educated young man and has patronage in America, but he is still … you know … I do not need to tell you that, do I?"

"Aadir is an Indian, I can see that, but at the same time he is different."

"Yes, his mother was a British girl who ran away with his Indian father, and at that time people were even more cruel than now, believe me. It was a disgrace for her family. They left India straight after their daughter ran away, but fortunately for the girl, she died giving birth to her son."

"Fortunately? Margaret, how can you say that!"

"She was abandoned by her own family and would not have been accepted by another Indian family. *What* do you think would have happened to her and her child? At least, from what I heard, the father of the child managed to return to his family and begged for forgiveness. Then he was married quickly and was allowed to keep the child."

Grace listened intently to Margaret. "That is a very tragic story, but thankfully with a happy ending for the child." She was amused how quickly Margaret had found out about Aadir.

"You might think this had a happy ending … but really stories like this never end. There are rules that must still be followed and you need to be very careful, my dear, very careful."

"I am not doing anything wrong, Margaret. For me, all people are the same and should have the same rights."

"Oh, my goodness, please do not say that out loud." Margaret slammed her teacup on the saucer. "I feel for you, I really do. I like you, Grace, and I am trying to help you as much as I can. I know he is attractive …"

"You mentioned a patron in America. How is that person linked to Aadir?"

"All I know is his name was Thomas. He was a civil engineer

who lived here for a long time and he was a cousin to that poor unfortunate girl, Aadir's mother. Thomas also left for America almost straight after that incident, for work reason. But he came back to India a few years later and offered his help to Kumar, Aadir's father. I was told that Thomas wanted to take care of Aadir in memory of his cousin. I do not know why, but perhaps he felt guilty about how her family had treated their daughter and left her behind. Anyway, who could say no to that offer? It was a winning lottery ticket and look at the result now. The boy has a chance in his life." Margaret filled up her cup with more tea.

"Now, coming back to reputation and connections. This is what I keep saying to you. Even though Aadir has a chance to enter our society, he will not be fully accepted. But because of Thomas, who has strong connections with the Colonel's family, he can join some of our events. Will he be accepted by others? I cannot tell you for sure. It is all about who you know, Grace. Remember that!"

That afternoon tea with Margaret stuck in Grace's head for some time. She couldn't stop thinking of Aadir and his family history. She felt sorry for his mother.

Grace and Aadir met briefly a few more times in the hotel. Margaret was always near and kept reminding Grace that she could not be seen with Aadir on her own. But once they managed to meet in the corner of a large park behind the hotel. Margaret was called out by one of her friends and Grace pretended that she was going to the ladies' room.

"Grace," began Aadir in his soft voice, melting her heart, "I don't want to get you into trouble. I know you cannot …"

"Aadir, it's fine," she stopped him. "It's my choice, but I don't want you to have troubles because of me either."

"You don't know about me. I have to tell you …"

She carefully touched the side of his arm with her hand "I know, Aadir."

"You know?"

"Sorry, in this society you can hardly hide anything. But it doesn't matter to me. May I ask, what was your mother's name?"

"Helen. You can ask me anything, Grace."

"Beautiful name. I am sorry, Aadir, to hear what happened to her. Did you know about her?"

"I only knew one mother. My father's wife. She was good to me and I loved her. She died when I was eighteen years old and was getting ready to go to America. That was when I found out about … Helen, my real mother."

Then Aadir explained about Thomas, who had helped Kumar financially with Aadir's education for all those years. When Grace listened to Aadir, she noticed that he was calm, not angry at all at his father or Thomas for not telling him the truth for so long. That was Aadir. She could see the gracious side of him. He was grateful to Thomas for his generosity and for taking care of him as if he were his own son.

Aadir told her that as soon as he had returned to India, his father began teaching him about the tea plantations. That included filling him in on the people he would have to deal with, which included James. Aadir admitted that, on the day they met, it was a great shock to find out that Grace was married, and not only married, but to James of all people. She was sure he had heard the rumours about her husband and his drinking and how she was barely able to leave the house. After all, who hadn't heard? And, again, with great delicacy, Aadir let her know that he understood her situation, that she was a lonely soul in a cruel position. Nobody could blame her. Grace felt like her heart was free. Now that Aadir knew everything, she could breathe. And what he had told her about his family, and especially about his mother, brought her closer to him. Grace also hadn't known about her parents and could feel for him. Her grandmother had kept her in the dark for many years and had probably taken some untold truths to her grave too. *Why is it that, in life, people keep secrets from each other?*

Aadir kept his gaze on Grace a little longer than usual and covered her hand with his own. "If you need anything, please let me know. Promise me, you will let me know." His eyes were full of tenderness.

She returned the same soft look on him. "I will. Thank you, Aadir."

"When will you be in Darjeeling?"

"Soon. Probably in two weeks' time. I am going with Margaret and her family. It will *just* be *me*." She knew that Aadir would understand her.

"I am leaving next week and will wait for you. Please be careful."

"I will and you too."

"How lucky I am to have met you. You are an exceptionally beautiful woman who deserves happiness. It's hard to leave you." He looked around over her head in concern, worried he had been overheard.

"Aadir …" She was overcome with shyness.

"I just wanted to express my admiration for you. You don't owe anyone anything, even me. I just feel good with you. I will do everything in my power to protect you. Please know that," he said to her, gently holding her hand.

There were no more words needed. That was enough for Grace to understand Aadir's feelings. It filled her with happiness and joy. She couldn't express her own feelings openly to him yet, but she felt the same.

Grace suddenly found herself in his arms. Aadir pressed her to his chest so gently she didn't resist. She rested her head on his shoulder and closed her eyes. It seemed to her, in that moment, that their hearts were beating in unison. She had found such peace and balance with him. It was as though he had opened doors into a world where there was no tension and pain, no fear, no lies, no tears. With him, she felt happy and content. Even when she had to say goodbye and return home, that peace and happiness went with her.

Darjeeling tea plantations

A new blend of tea and love

Darjeeling was one of the preferable destinations for British officers and their wives to spend summers. The air was brisk and cool in the foothills of the Himalayan mountains. Lord Clifford himself told Grace that, when he started his tea business, the first thing he did was to buy a house in Darjeeling. The house was almost on the top of a hill and was secluded and surrounded by trees which provided a lot of shade for both it and the garden. It became the Clifford summer residence in Darjeeling. Grace personally thanked her father-in-law in a letter for the opportunity to spend summers in such a stunning place and escape the stifling heat in Calcutta. She was also happy that Margaret and her family also stayed in Darjeeling for the summers. They spent a lot of time together. Hannah had developed asthma and the mountain air was just what she needed. This summer, however, Grace would spend without Margaret, who was taking Hannah to England. She didn't say much to Grace but warned her that times were changing. Grace hadn't paid much attention to the political situation in India at that time. All her thoughts were with Aadir.

She loved spending time in Darjeeling near the tea plantations. The house was a bungalow, but much bigger than the one they had in Calcutta. There were more rooms with more light. The interior had calming colours on the walls, and there was a piano. For Grace this was an absolute treasure. The big garden was full of shrubs and marigolds that lined the path leading towards the tea plantations with the forest behind them. Grace sipped her tea slowly, sitting in the corner of the verandah, where the aroma of jasmine bushes was strong. She looked far into the distance and kept her gaze on one spot. Somewhere there, behind the trees, where the hill ended and at the bottom of the tea plantations, was the house of the Gupta family. Kumar, as a tea plantation manager, had always lived there. Grace wondered if Aadir had already arrived.

James had told her that he wouldn't be around for some time, but promised he would soon be stationed at another place near Darjeeling. Then they would spend more time together. Grace would have preferred him to stay where he was. The less they saw of each other the better. She was tired of pretending in public that they were still a happily married couple. She wanted to go back to England as soon as possible. Her nana had been right when she said that she was lucky to have avoided that debauched and vulgar life the British wives and their husbands lived in India. Grace, now, saw it with her own eyes. But James told her she couldn't leave India. It could harm his reputation if his wife left without him. He told her that she was stuck with him, like it or not. So, it would be better if she sat tight and acted happy, as she had everything she needed. But now, since meeting Aadir, she had changed her mind. Grace had started to think it would be better if her husband left her and that she actually wouldn't mind staying in India.

Grace chose to sleep in the corner room this time, which had a door opening straight into the garden, not the bedroom she stayed in last time. Only Grace and Zia understood the real attraction of this room.

Lord Clifford had stopped coming to India some time ago, delegating the responsibilities of the tea supply to Oliver. Grace couldn't wait to see Molly, but last year Oliver had come without her and it seemed this time he would be coming alone again. Family business had kept Molly at home since Grace had moved to India. Molly's letters were very brief. Grace could sense how upset her friend was that she couldn't come to India with her husband. Grace wanted to share her new feelings towards Aadir with Molly, but alas there was another summer ahead without her dear friend.

Grace and Aadir understood the risk they were taking, but they couldn't resist each other's company. Grace let herself dive into her new feelings, not thinking about what would happen afterwards. The thought of what Helen must have felt when she met Aadir's father fired her imagination. She could see how destiny might repeat itself. Both she and Aadir just wanted to enjoy each other's company under the warm rays of the sun on freshly cut grass, or under the bright moon. Nobody could disturb their idyll. They were well hidden from prying eyes. Zia managed to create all kinds of cover for them.

She had no doubts that it was love – deep and real. An invisible, powerful affinity connected them. Sometimes, the feeling was so strong, Grace was overwhelmed by it. Aadir was always careful and gentle. As time passed, Grace stopped being tense and anxious, things she always felt when she was with James. She felt no guilt, trusting Aadir with all her heart. She would stay in India forever if it meant being with him. If necessary, she would run away with him, anywhere, so that James couldn't find her. For the first time in her life, she felt so brave. Aadir's love had changed her, making her more sensitive, more feminine. She finally opened up and allowed Aadir to see how she felt. They woke up every morning with one desire: to see each other.

Grace would sometimes wear a sari and cover her head to hide herself when she was outside the house. They even managed to meet in town a few times. Nobody recognised her. Zia, of course, would accompany her. It was a new way for her to explore the life and culture of the local community in Darjeeling. The town was famous for its artistic handicrafts and its traditional colour designs. Grace also loved the hill walks, from where she could observe the magnificent Himalayan mountains. The peaks were covered with snow like sugar loaves. She was fascinated and magnetised by them. They both enjoyed their time together, but, although Grace wore her sari when they were in town, Aadir admitted that he worried somebody would recognise her. It was better not to take such a risk. She agreed.

The summer of 1946 had passed very quickly. September was more pleasant, not too hot. One night, Aadir managed to sneak into Grace's room unnoticed and brought her a bouquet of fresh flowers. She was waiting for him. Aadir had only two seconds to put the flowers down on the table next to the door after he entered the room, before they flew into each other's arms. First, he kissed her gently on both cheeks, then her lips, her hair and eyes. Then Aadir kissed her more passionately. She could feel they were both hungry for love, for being together, just the two of them in their own world. Grace was bursting with desire for Aadir. Her pulse pounded. Although no words were spoken between them, their bodies clearly agreed they had waited for this moment for long enough.

He stopped kissing her and whispered in her ear that she looked amazing with her eyes shining. She whispered back that he made them shine. He caressed her hair, smelled it, and then his hand moved slowly down to her neck and back. Grace looked into his eyes, drowning in their depths, full of passion and tenderness for her. It was easy to see into his soul through his eyes, as the doors were open, their sparkle shining brightly showing the way to the world he was prepared to take her to. She was not afraid. His eyes were perfectly mapped with mandala, like that ancient Indian art symbolising of protection. And she felt protected. She took his hand and put it on her chest where her heart was and pulled him towards her. They took a few steps together. By the time they reached the edge of the bed, they were ready to fall on it, but Aadir stopped.

"I love you, Grace. I've loved you with all my heart from that first moment I saw you." He held her waist with one hand and put his other on her cheek like he was holding a fragile rosebud. His gaze was the most tender and loving. It was the first time in her life Grace had heard these words. Her husband had never told her that he loved her. *It is probably meant to be*, she quickly thought. When Aadir said these words, they sounded like magic. They were not just words. They travelled deep inside her, touching every part of her body. They meant the world to her and rooted in her mind and heart straight away. She was accepted. She was respected and loved by a man she also loved. It was true, unconditional love. It was worth waiting for.

"I love you, Aadir! And I, too, probably fell in love with you on our first meeting."

"Probably?"

"I am just teasing you." She looked at him with a cheeky smile.

He kissed her tenderly and whispered, "I don't want to hurt you."

Grace understood what Aadir meant. They had spoken about it before. She knew that they wouldn't be allowed to get married in India even after she managed to get divorced from James. Hindu law prohibited Hindus from marrying non-Hindus. To be together, they were considering other countries like England or America, where Aadir had lived before and where he'd have the chance to go back, according to Thomas. She knew that Aadir was a true gentleman and he would never take advantage of her. He treasured her feelings for him and was very delicate with her. She kissed him back the same way he had kissed her, slowly, with tenderness.

"You won't hurt me, Aadir. It's my decision also."

Then she started to unbutton the top of her dress. She closed her eyes and Aadir took over, opening the remaining buttons. The dress dropped to the floor. Once Grace was standing in front of him naked, he quickly got undressed himself and they fell into bed. She circled his neck with her arms, but before she could kiss him, Aadir said, "Grace, if anything separates us … I will find you. Please remember that. I will never let anything or anybody hurt you."

"I know." She sent him a loving smile.

"Ah, that smile of yours." Aadir kissed her on the corners of her lips. She smiled again. "My love, don't tease me or I will kiss you all night." He touched her chin with two fingers, admiring her features and searching where to kiss next. After a few more caresses, Grace laid her head on his chest.

"You are so fragile, but I want to hug you so tightly." He gently embraced Grace and held her in his arms, then buried his nose in her hair, which had the scent of wild flowers and tea leaves. It seemed to her that in that moment they both understood they would always be together, no matter what. Their souls united and created a beautiful aura around them, a world where there were only the two of them, a world full of happiness and love. They were so content and blessed in that moment. He stroked her body with a touch like silk. Extraordinary sensations spread everywhere over her skin.

"Thank you for allowing me to love you." Aadir's deeptimbred voice echoed in her ears. She cried out for more. She was melting under his caresses. He guided her slowly and his every move was so gentle that Grace almost screamed. She had never experienced such wonderful contentment. They made passionate love full of tenderness and their mutual hunger was way beyond the physical. Time came to a standstill. Their bodies merged, moving in rhythm, taking them on a journey of divine discovery. While their bodies were lost in bliss, their souls were creating their own mandala – an eternal love between them.

A change of plans

Lives deviated

In the early hours of the following morning, Grace and Aadir were still embracing, caution far from their thoughts, when they heard the sound of loud voices and a roar. Grace could recognise James's voice in her sleep. Icy coldness seeped into her veins.

"It's him … Aadir, you need to leave. Hurry."

In seconds, Aadir was picking up his clothes from the floor. He was about to leave when he rushed back and hugged her.

"Everything will be fine," he whispered. "Stay calm, my love. I will be back for you." He looked straight at her and gently pressed his lips on hers, then flew out the door that led to the garden. When Aadir was gone, Grace, with the speed of light, put on her nightdress and returned to bed.

It was still half dark outside. Grace hoped Aadir would be careful, that he wouldn't be spotted by the plantation workers, who would have already arrived. The servants of the house, too, would no doubt have been awakened by James's noisy entrance. Aadir needed to leave with extra caution this time.

She had barely had time to think when James burst into the room like a demented bull. Grace sat up in bed, clutching the sheet in her hands and trembling all over with fear.

"I didn't find you in your bedroom. Why are you here? He peeked around the room, frowning. Then he studied her face with concern in his eyes.

"I … James … I didn't know you were coming. I always sleep here when I'm painting." A shiver ran all over her body.

"Painting? I see…" He glanced over at the table covered in painting supplies. The flowers were gone. She released a big sigh of relief. Aadir took the flowers with him. *Gosh, when did he have the time to think of it?*

Grace heard Oliver's voice somewhere in the house, but before she could ask any questions, James slammed the door behind him. She understood he had decided to stay with her in this room. Her brain worked fast. She realised that the other side of the bed might still be warm from Aadir's body and moved quickly to that side. Without another word, James threw off his clothes and collapsed onto the bed next to Grace. She was still sitting up, her body covered with the sheet.

"It is good to be in a warm bed with my wife," muttered James. He turned to give her a grin. When he put his hand on her shoulder, she didn't move at first, but as she didn't want to make him angry, she then lay down on her back. She waited in fear for what would come next. Just a few minutes earlier, Aadir had been lying next to her. Now James lay there, like he had always been there. Frantically, she tried to think of what she should do. Had Aadir managed to return to his house unnoticed? What would happen tomorrow? Had any of the workers seen him? Where was Zia? Why hadn't she woken them up? The questions, one after another, overwhelmed her.

Within five minutes James was snoring. He reeked of alcohol, as usual. She could smell the slight scent of Aadir on her pillow. James had a stuffy nose when he was drunk, so he wouldn't catch any scent on the bed. Grace couldn't sleep at all. Dawn was the darkest time of all for her. She wanted to disappear into that darkness like snow melting in the sun.

The next day, the house was quiet. James and Oliver spent most of it on the plantations, interacting with the workers and Kumar. Oliver told her that he had come to secure the probable export of the batch of tea. She couldn't understand what he meant by that but decided to talk to Oliver later. Her mind was somewhere else. As far as she could see, there was no sign of trouble for her and Aadir. She sat quietly in the garden, staring at the white canvas in front of her. Her hands were stiff, but she forced herself to run her brushes over the surface, to at least make it look like she was painting.

"Sahib is only here for a couple of days." It was Zia, whispering in her ear. "Fresh lemonade, memsahib." And she placed a glass on the table beside Grace.

"Are you sure, Zia? He will leave?"

"I heard, memsahib, that sahib has to return to his regiment for duty."

Late in the afternoon, Grace was still in the garden, still pretending to paint. This time it was Oliver who approached her with news. He needed to leave for a neighbouring village to secure some extra labour, he said. He promised that he would be back before James left the following morning. Grace closed her eyes and raised her face to the sky. She whispered a prayer to herself. Just one night, one more night and she would be free.

That evening, James was even drunker than usual. When he left the house, she hoped he wouldn't return until morning. She hadn't seen Aadir all day and wanted to go to bed alone, thinking about him. She was in her room, standing in front of the mirror in her nightgown, combing her hair, when James came in quietly behind her and put his hands on her shoulders. Grace screamed. James quickly placed his hand over her lips and she turned towards him. He looked at her with piercing eyes. His gaze wandered all over her face and body, the muscles in his jaw tightening. He was furious, but as he always liked to, he was deliberately delaying whatever he planned to do. He took a lock of her hair in his hand, turned it, then pulled it down.

Grace tilted her head away from him. She closed her eyes as James's other hand gripped her forearm so tightly that she bit her tongue. The smell of alcohol filled the entire room. Grace wanted to turn away, she was choking on the unbearable fumes of whiskey and cigars. He continued to squeeze her arms, his fingers digging into her skin like nails into wood. Grace bit her lip and made a strangled sound.

"Please, James … stop it," she managed. "You are hurting me. I don't want this. Please … let me go!" Though she hadn't yet opened her eyes, she could feel him staring at her. *Did he find out about me and Aadir?*

James hadn't touched her for a long time. They had managed to communicate and tolerate each other's company, but they weren't close at all. What was happening today? Grace didn't know what to do. Her body was tense and, from past experience, could tell what was coming, but although she knew him, James was unpredictable. What could be worse than what he had already done to her? If he had found out about her and Aadir, then why wasn't he saying anything? She expected his accusations, his rejection, which would lead to a divorce. That was what she really wanted to happen. But James neither uttered a word nor accused her of being unfaithful. The next thing she saw were his eyes flashing with anger and his face above hers.

It was quick and ugly. If before he had been violent with her, this time it went beyond anything she could imagine. On every part of her body, he touched, he left a bruise. His eyes were burning with inner anger, but he said nothing as he assaulted her. On top of her was an animal, not a man. Her body went into such shock that she couldn't even feel pain. She fought her tears, pushing them back and swallowing them.

Afterwards Grace lay on her back next to him, struggling to move a finger. She heard him getting up, in silence. He tried to find his clothes on the floor, swear words coming out of his mouth to hang in the air like poison. She held her breath, only exhaling once he left the room. For a few more minutes, she could hear the sound of him staggering around the house until he finally got into his room.

Grace pulled her knees up to her chin. She lay half naked on the bed, in tears. Not only had her nightgown been torn apart that night but her marriage too. Blood flowed down her legs. She didn't make a sound so as not to frighten anyone in the house. She wanted to die. She was humiliated and destroyed, as a woman, as a wife, as a person. Grace was so ashamed that she was afraid to call Zia. She felt that she had lost her dignity.

In the semi-darkness she managed to get to the bathroom with the help of Zia, who had slipped into her room quietly. Zia was whispering in her ear that she would look after her as she washed Grace and changed her clothes. Grace wouldn't get back into the bed where *that* just happened. One of her arms barely moved and was very sore. Her legs felt so heavy.

Zia carefully laid her on the sofa in the room and covered her with a blanket, murmuring under her breath, “There is a lot of bad energy inside him, very bad. Evil energy will destroy its master one day. It will destroy him!”

Zia managed to bring Grace herbal tea to soothe her pain. She was such an angel. But the moment of peace was short.

“Memsahib, wake up. Please wake up. Are you all right, memsahib?” Grace opened her eyes. Zia was standing over her. “Your things are packed, memsahib. The car is ready. Sahib is waiting for you.”

“What? I don’t understand.” She reached for Zia’s hand. “Is he still here?”

“You have been very ill last night. Delirious and with a fever, even in your sleep. Sahib said he couldn’t leave you in such a condition.”

Grace looked towards the bed. It had been changed and there was no sign of the bloodstained sheets.

“Don’t worry, memsahib. No one saw anything; I took care of it all. I will come with you too. Sahib doesn’t mind. He actually insisted I come with you.”

“Come where? Where is he taking us?”

Zia shook her head. It seemed to Grace she might cry.

“I don’t know, memsahib. I don’t know where. We must go or sahib will get angry again.”

"Is Oliver in the house?" Grace tried to hang on to any possibility of staying and asking for help, but it was one of those days when she had been left alone.

"No, memsahib, he is not."

"I suppose we are going back to Calcutta."

"Perhaps. All the things are packed. I will just help you to get dressed, memsahib."

Grace raised herself unsteadily onto her feet, her face pale. She allowed Zia to help her dress, and with fists clenched to overcome the pain, she faced her husband outside the house. Zia quickly walked ahead to the car with Grace's belongings. James stood there smoking in a pose full of arrogance.

Passing him, Grace whispered, "If you ever touch me again … it will be the last time … for both of us."

Out of the corner of her eye she noticed a change in his gaze. He froze for a moment with his cigar stuck between two fingers. His clenched jaw and the thunder in his eyes indicated that he was angry, but he was surprised too. He hadn't been expecting her to be brave enough to speak to him after what happened last night, especially in such a calm tone. Her whispering had actually had a stronger effect than if she had shouted at him.

Grace thought, *If I can stay and wait for Oliver, I could ask for his help. Or I could run, but where?* Her brain went through different ways she might save herself from her violent husband, but in the end, she couldn't do anything. She simply didn't have the energy to fight him and was ashamed, blaming herself for allowing James to drag her into his life. Now, it was too late. She also didn't want to make a lot of noise because of Aadir. She didn't want him to be involved in her troubles with James. Each step towards the car was extremely painful for her. But the pain was not physical, it came from the thought that soon she would be far from Aadir. The only hope she had was that he would find her later and together they would think of something. And Zia was with her. Everything would be fine.

From sweet to sour

New hopes

Grace opened her eyes wide when she saw where James had taken her. In front of them was an old house with the Himalayas in the background and an endless forest of trees. She had slept on the journey, but she didn't think they had driven for too long. So, this place wouldn't be too far from Darjeeling, then. It was some time in the evening, but still bright.

"Where are we? What are we doing here?"

"I'm stationed here for now. All you need to know is that you will stay in this house while I'm on duty."

"Why?"

"Why? You are my wife! What a stupid question."

"For how long?"

"You ask too many questions." He started to get irritated. Grace didn't have the energy to argue. He began walking towards the house, opened the door and went in. Grace and Zia followed.

The singlestorey house was in good condition and fully

furnished, but it was clear that nobody had lived there for some time. James pointed towards one of the bedrooms in the long corridor and said Grace could take that one. There was a sitting room with French doors opening onto a big verandah with a picturesque view over the mountains. Grace stood in the middle of the room for a moment staring at the view, but she didn't feel any joy. The house walls had no pictures on them apart from a big one hanging over the sofa with the English countryside on it. When Grace walked into the dining room her eyes immediately fell on the big wooden table in the middle of the room. It was carved in the shape of an elephant and each of the six chairs around it were fashioned into a throne. She was still half asleep and tired from their journey, so she stared at the table trying to imagine herself eating at it every day from now on.

"It was Major Spencer's sister's house. They left a few months back to return to England and kindly offered me their house."

Grace didn't say anything.

"There is a small town and a few shops, but I would advise you to stay at home for a while. It's not safe out there."

How kind of him to show that he cares for me, thought Grace. Was it safe being with him under the same roof? He hadn't cared about her last night. Despite being married to James for three years now, Grace still couldn't get used to how quickly he could change from a kind man into an abusive one. She put her left hand on her right arm and closed her eyes for a second. The sharp pain pierced her arm and travelled up to her shoulder. He had squeezed her arm last night so tightly that she could barely move it now.

"Is there a room for Zia?"

"Yes, she can take the annex behind the kitchen. There are two boys in the house at your disposal. If you need anything, you can send me a message through one of them."

"I don't know this house and…"

"Believe me," he interrupted her. "I, myself, can't wait to get out of this shithole, but we are here, for now. I can't tell you for how long. Things are unsettled in India at the moment. We might leave next year in spring or summer."

"You mean leave this place?"

"India!"

"India?" Grace asked this a bit too emotionally. She coughed to cover it up.

"What? Have you already changed your mind and would now like to stay here for longer? I remember you were complaining about the heat when we arrived."

"Are you saying we are going back to England next year?"

"Possibly. We'll see."

On the way out, he said, "There is enough food for now. I have to go. Don't wait for me for dinner." He looked in the mirror on the wall, sorting his hair.

Grace decided not to ask more questions, at least, not now. Her head was splitting; her whole body ached and reminded her of what had happened last night. The shock of where she had ended up had distracted her, but now the pain came back. She wanted to be left alone. *Let him go away*, she said to herself. She just wanted him to leave. When James was gone and Zia had put down fresh sheets on her new bed in somebody else's house, Grace lay down and fell asleep almost immediately.

When she got up, she found that Zia had already prepared the house well. The rooms had been tidied and, in the kitchen, water was boiling in huge pails over a brightly burning fire. Grace asked Zia to find out as much as she could about this place. Maybe there was a way to get a message to Aadir. She had woken to the awful realisation that Aadir had no way of knowing where she was.

"Unfortunately, memsahib," Zia said, as though reading her mind, "there is no way of sending a letter to anyone without sahib knowing about it." Then Zia added that the servants were under James's command and Zia wasn't allowed to go outside the main town gate.

"We are here … alone, memsahib," said Zia in her sad voice. "Only the mountains around us."

"So, you have no idea where we are?"

Zia shook her head. "No, memsahib, but I will do my best to find out. I just need time."

"Thanks, Zia. What would I do without you."

A month later, Zia managed to get the information for Grace when she went for groceries. The town they lived in was called Kurseong. It was only thirty kilometres from Darjeeling. Grace couldn't believe that she wasn't far away from Aadir. She began to think how she could send a letter to him. She hadn't heard anything from him since she had left and had even begun to doubt his feelings for her, even though she knew he wouldn't have been able to find out where she was. It wasn't too long before Zia found a way to send a message. One of the local boys had a relative working on the Darjeeling tea plantations and he was planning to visit him. Grace was cautious and wrote only Aadir's name and her location in the message. She had no idea what Aadir could or would do, but at least he would know where she was. To Grace's great disappointment, a week later Zia learned from the boy that nobody was there to receive Grace's message. Zia said that she had tried to describe Kumar as well as Aadir, but the boy said he didn't see either of them. Neither Kumar nor Aadir remained on the plantations.

Almost two months later, Grace started to hear the beats of two hearts inside her. She had suspected it before, but now she knew it for sure. She was pregnant. Her body was changing. The nausea had only grown worse. When she told Zia, her maid gave Grace a big smile and said that she had figured it out. Grace's eating habits had changed and a natural blush had appeared on her face again.

"I'm so happy for you, memsahib. New life is good."

"Thank you, Zia. I don't know what to feel. I mean I'm excited, but I'm nervous too."

"All will be good, memsahib, all will be good. No need to worry."

Grace didn't say what was really worrying her. She knew Zia would understand that too. James hadn't approached her since that night on the plantations, as he was on duty all the time and had probably taken her words seriously this time. All her thoughts now were about the baby. *Oh,* she said fearfully to herself, *who is the father of the baby?* She realised that she couldn't be sure and that doubt hurt her deeply. It stopped her searching for the way to contact Aadir. It changed *everything*. She felt lost for a while, but she managed to get herself together and started to make a plan in her head. She knew if Aadir was the father of her baby, it would be obvious, and James wouldn't like it. He would leave her. That was what she wanted. Then she would go to Calcutta, find Aadir and tell him about their child. *But what if James is the baby's father?* That thought was harder to accept. In that case, she would never see Aadir again. With all the stress and uncertainty, Grace decided to wait until after the birth of the baby to work out what she should do.

Another two months passed before Grace managed to tell her husband the news. Her pregnancy was just starting to show. She was waiting in the sitting room when James came back home and she blurted it out before he had even come through the doorway.

"James, I'm … expecting a child." She stood up and paused. "I know how much you have wanted this." She nervously glanced at him. She couldn't help babbling. Why was he standing there, frozen, and why was he looking at her in that way?

"I'm actually quite far gone," she continued, as he walked slowly into the sitting room and poured himself a whiskey. "I will have to see a doctor soon to make sure everything is all right."

James walked across the room, from one corner to the other. He looked, perturbed, at Grace before turning away from her and asking about the duration of her pregnancy. He took a sip of whiskey before she replied.

"I think over four months." Grace's voice trembled.

"Over four months? And you are just *now* telling me this?" James looked at his wife as he circled her. "Mind you, I can see it now. I thought you had just gained weight." He gave her a crooked smile.

"I didn't know how to tell you … You have been away and busy. When can I see a doctor?"

After a few seconds he replied, "I will arrange that."

"Thank you. Will you take me to the hospital?"

"The doctor will come here."

"Here? But …"

"I *said* the doctor will see you here, in the house."

"I will need to go to hospital when it is due." Grace gently placed her hand on her rounded belly.

"Believe me, this house is far safer than any hospital in this godforsaken country. There are rats running around in the hospitals. That is what you want, the company of rats?"

James emptied his glass of whiskey in one gulp and banged it down on the table. He started heading for the door. She could see this conversation was annoying him, but she couldn't let it go.

"James, we can't risk our baby's safety."

"*Our* baby?" James turned around and glared at Grace like he was working something out in his head. She just about managed to hold his gaze. His eyes were cold and alien. "Then it's up to me to decide." With that, James left the room, slamming the door behind him.

Left alone with her worries, Grace stroked her belly and tried to calm herself down. She was unable to assimilate her new reality at that moment. With a sour taste in her mouth and fear stuck in her throat, she managed to think about the new life growing inside her, which was changing her in more significant way. She already knew it didn't matter who the father of her child was; she loved her child and couldn't wait for the day she would meet him.

After that conversation, fruit began to appear more often in the house, as well as many other treats. James even took Grace to the mountains a couple of times, which were incredibly beautiful. She was surprised, but grateful for such moments. She decided not to argue with her husband anymore and not to spoil the good times he allowed her to have there. A British doctor was visiting her from time to time. He was in his late sixties and told her that he had lived there for as long as he could remember. He never married and intend to stay in India. Grace noticed that sometimes she could smell alcohol on him. The doctor himself didn't look healthy, but James said he was the only British doctor available in this town.

The cool mountain air was a delight for her. She plumped up the cushion on one of the soft armchairs and slowly placed her heavy body in it. The view from their verandah was amazing, especially in the evening. She was just about to raise her cup of tea to her lips when Zia appeared in front of her, out of breath.

"What is it, Zia? Have you been chased by someone?"

"Sorry, memsahib, I am afraid I have news you are not going to like."

"Well, let's hear it then."

Zia peeked around. "Memsahib, the boy I befriended, from the town … he told me …"

"You don't need to worry, just say it."

"He said that Aadir … got married." She tried to hide her eyes.

"Aadir? Married?" Faded thoughts of Aadir rushed into her head, giving her a sharp sensation. She lifted her hands and pressed her temples with her fingers. After many months of waiting, she had already accepted that Aadir wasn't searching for her, but she didn't expect to hear news about his marriage. So, that was it. She felt a sudden kick inside her, which brought her back to thoughts of her child. Her belly had grown big. She gently put her hand on it.

"Memsahib, are you feeling well? Water? Or maybe lemonade?"

"I'm all right, thank you, Zia." She was still slightly doubtful, and surprised herself when she asked, "How does that boy know?"

"Mr Gupta was briefly at the plantations, and somebody overheard him talking about his son's wedding. He couldn't stop saying how beautiful it was, full of … Oh, sorry, memsahib, I don't know anything more. Just this."

Grace glanced towards the white peaks of the mountains far away and exhaled weakly. For a while a deadly silence fell. Zia patiently waited.

"Did you manage to buy lavender on the market?" Grace deliberately changed the subject. She didn't want to show Zia how upsetting the news was for her.

"Yes, memsahib, yes. I make sure you have fresh lavender under your pillow tonight. Fresh, very fresh, how you like it."

Soon after that, when Grace was just over eight months pregnant, a sharp pain suddenly pierced her belly. She called for Zia. From the sofa where she lay, Grace watched Zia scribble a note and give it to the houseboy, ordering him to run as fast as possible to get to James. Zia had told her she had no experience in delivering babies but had once witnessed her grandmother do it. Grace watched Zia running around the house gathering clean sheets and towels while muttering a prayer under her breath. It was obvious she was frightened but trying hard not to let Grace see this.

"All will be good, memsahib. Please try not to worry, memsahib. Doctor is coming. I will make your favourite tea."

The image of her mother delivering her under the hawthorn tree came to Grace's mind. If her mother had done it, so could she. She took a few deep breaths. Her sudden panic attack subsided. Zia helped Grace to move to her bedroom where she spent some time in peace, sipping herbal tea. The lavender smell under her pillow also helped her to relax. Then she felt a kick inside her, then another one. The cramps were coming faster. Grace screamed. When she cried out, Zia rushed into the room. Zia was trembling all over, the fear so strong that her hands were shaking. She was trying to tell Grace something.

"Sahib and the doctor have arrived. The doctor doesn't look too good, memsahib, not good, he is drunk again. They argued. Sahib is angry. I didn't hear anything; I didn't hear anything."

"Zia, what is happening? I can't understand what you are trying to say."

"Sahib said to the doctor…" In that moment James and the doctor walked in.

What Zia wanted to tell Grace remained a mystery.

Coming back home

Lost and broken

The first thing Grace saw when she opened her eyes was James. He had a strange look on his face, hard to read. Her eyelids were heavy, as though her body didn't want to obey her anymore. Her head buzzed. All she could register, besides James's presence, was the outline of someone else, standing behind him. Grace tried to speak, but the sound that came out was incomprehensible, even to her, and she fell back into unconsciousness.

When she opened her eyes a second time, there was no one in the room. Grace stared at the ceiling for a long time, trying to remember where she was. A strong smell of lavender brought her gaze to the side of the bed. *Why is lavender all over my bed and not in the sachet under the pillow?* Gradually her head began to clear, and Grace abruptly jumped up.

"My baby. Where is my baby?"

Then she put her hands on her stomach and screamed. James came to her side, followed by the doctor. The two of them began to comfort her.

“Doctor, where is my baby? James?!”

“You need to calm down, darling.” He put both of his hands on her arm, then turned to the doctor. “Hurry man, get on with it,” he growled.

The doctor was drawing some kind of liquid into a syringe. His hands were shaking. James leaned over and gently kissed her on her forehead. It was a distraction. Grace only understood this when the doctor injected the substance into her arm. Warmth rushed through her veins and her tension subsided. James touched Grace’s hair softly. She closed her eyes. The last words she heard were between James and the doctor.

“I can’t lose her…”

“She will be fine. Will I get my…?”

“Shut up and just do what I told you. You will get it after you do it.”

In the hours and days that followed, Grace drifted in and out of sleep. Fragments of what James had told her came back. She had almost died, he said, on account of all the blood she had lost. Unfortunately, the child couldn’t be saved. The baby didn’t breathe after leaving her body. The doctor had done what was needed to save Grace’s life. She had been delirious for five days after the birth. Did her baby really die? She had never got the chance to see him. It was a boy James told her, and he reminded her that the child was his son as well as hers. He had done his best to save both his wife and their son. He had saved her. James looked like he was grieving, but Grace didn't believe him.

Grace spent most of the journey from India to England in a semi-conscious state. The sea was rough and she felt a slight swaying that lulled her even more. Her left arm was sore from the needle that had been injected into her skin so often. It was probably James who made sure she was sedated for so much of the time. When the ship's doctor visited her, she tried to question him, but he didn't know anything.

"My wife is in mourning," James told him. "Our child was lost at birth and she's in a very bad way." He was at her side all the time and prevented Grace from talking to anybody on her own. The doctor assured Grace that she had avoided the worst that could have happened.

"In India, many people are dying because of infection," he said. "Rest is what you need, Mrs Clifford. I'm sure the future will bring you more children. Now, you need to take care of yourself."

She silently agreed with the doctor by closing her eyes. She didn't move and continued sitting on the sofa. When the doctor left, James followed him to the door. Her thoughts kept bringing her back to that house. Where was Zia? Grace didn't see her before they left, and she didn't say goodbye. That made her very sad. There was no one around Grace felt she could talk to or trust. Each day on the ship, taking her away from India, from Aadir and her son, was like a small death.

Grace sensed a light aroma of lavender coming from somewhere near her. She stood up and slowly walked from the sofa to the desk in the cabin. The smell followed her. She put her hand in the pocket of her dress, where she felt something inside it. There it was. The sachet of lavender Zia usually put under her pillow. She was glad to see it. At least there was something Grace could now hold in her hand that would remind her of the night her son was born. Then she remembered the scent of lavender on her bed. So, the sachet must be empty then? She opened it and … froze.

Tears poured down her cheeks when she slowly took a small lock of soft dark hair out of the lavender sachet. It was tied with one of the red threads Zia would use in her knitting. Grace's heart sank. The sachet fell on the floor. Placing the lock of hair in the palm of her hand, she looked at it, biting her lower lip. It was so tiny. She then brought it up to her lips and closed her eyes. Grace's whole body trembled from the silent sobbing inside her. It was her son's hair.

Part III

England 1947–1969

London, Spring 1947

Time for grieving

Upon arriving home in England, Grace's devastation and frustration brought her to the state of mind of being completely lost. She didn't know where she was, she couldn't eat and barely slept. One night she found herself in the garden in her nightgown. She was filled with pain and sorrow, and silently, stood there in the rain, water dripping down her hair to her face, shoulders and arms. The sudden thirst in her dry mouth forced her to lift her face up and she started to swallow the rain drops, barely tasting the cold water running down her parched throat. Her body was numb. She wanted her troubled life to turn into dust and then be washed away with the rain. Bereft of love she felt empty. Would she ever taste life again?

Next morning, she woke up, but kept her eyes closed for some time as her eyelids were heavy. When she slowly opened them, she saw a silhouette of somebody against the light from the window, sitting next to her bed.

"Molly?" Grace tried to get up on her elbows.

"Yes, it's me," Molly said softly and leaned into Grace to

hug her. They stayed in each other's arms for a while, both crying.

"I'm so sorry, Grace. I can't even imagine what you have been through, but I'm glad you are home now." Molly kissed Grace on the cheek and wiped her tears with the handkerchief she held.

"I'm so happy to see you, Molly. Where am I?"

"You are at home. James's house in London."

"Why London? I want to go to White Cliffs." Grace moved into a sitting position in bed with Molly's help.

"James said that he has to be in London. What I know from Oliver is that James is sorting his affairs after leaving India. He's a retired officer now."

"What does that mean?"

"His military career has ended and he needs to find a job. From what I know, James is not happy about it. He's arguing with Oliver and their father all the time. He wants to join the family business, but Lord Clifford doesn't have a position for him after having lost his business in Darjeeling. India got its independence and that has affected many British businesses there. Times have changed, Grace, for all of us. At least the war is over, but there is a lot to be done in the country."

"I want to go home, my home." Grace looked down at the handkerchief in her hands, then used it to wipe away a tear on her cheek. Molly put her hand on Grace's arm.

"I know. I know how you feel, but James …"

"I'm leaving him."

"What to do you *mean* leaving?"

"I don't want to see him again. I want a divorce."

"Divorce? Grace, I understand what you feel right now. You are exhausted. Please wait until …"

"Until what?"

"You can't be on your own right now."

"Why not? I want to be on my own. I don't want to see him anymore. I can't stand him!" Grace dropped her face into her hands, crying again.

Molly was silent for a moment, then said, "Grace, I'm here to help you. You are not well and need to see a doctor."

"I don't need a doctor. I want to be left alone."

"All right, as you wish. I will come back later." Molly got up.

"Molly, I didn't mean you. I'm … I don't know … I can't do this anymore … My baby. They took my baby away. I didn't see my baby, my son! Molly, *he* took my son away from me!"

"Oh, Grace, sweetheart." Molly leaned over and gently pulled Grace's head towards her shoulder, whispering, "I'm so sorry for your loss. I *feel* for you. Cry. Sometimes it helps. Cry. I understand and wish I had been there for you."

"I waited for you. I missed you so much!"

"I missed you too! There is so much to tell you, but not now."

"I'm tired. I constantly feel tired."

"You have been through a lot. Of course, you feel tired. It's natural being stressed and worried in your situation, but try to stay focused."

"Focused on what, Molly?"

"Life goes on, Grace. I know it's too early maybe, but it's better not to dwell on the past now. It will only make you more miserable. You have us all to support you."

"I'm not sure. Is there life without my son? I want to go back. I want to find him."

"Grace, your son is buried in India. Try … to accept it. Maybe one day you can go back to India and visit his grave."

"You think that one day I will be able to do this?"

"Who knows, maybe. You have to have hope – the purpose of life."

"I am in pain all over. I don't know how I will continue to live. I'm afraid when my pain goes away, I will lose myself."

"Oh, dear. Grace, you don't need to punish yourself like this. Please stay calm with a clear mind. We are all here for you."

"I don't want to be here. I would rather *die* than live with *him* under the same roof."

"What happened in India? I can see you are very angry with James. He is maybe not the best husband, but to think of dying … Where is my strong and passioned Grace? You always had a zest for life. Did you leave that Grace behind in India?"

"I probably left her there." Grace gave Molly a crooked smile, then quickly switched to a look of concern. "I need to tell you something."

"Look, James is coming back soon. You can tell me all about your life in India next time. I have to go. I am sorry."

"Molly, please don't leave me."

"I'm not leaving you. I will be back. You better get yourself together and accept help. You can rely on me and Oliver. You are not alone, but please, for now, keep your mind away from thoughts of leaving James. You need to stay calm and take care of yourself. You don't want to be locked up in one of those mental hospitals, do you?"

"Mental hospital? Is that where he wants to send me?"

"No, no! Sorry I said that. Just stay calm and see a doctor. You are crying all the time and not eating properly. What do you think it looks like?"

"I have seen enough doctors. Look at my arms, all bruised from needles." She pulled her nightgown's sleeves up.

"My goodness! Grace, your arms are blue!"

"I told you."

"It looks awful, but from what I learned, the doctor tried to save your life. I can't even imagine what could have happened if you had got an infection or something else there. I know somebody who lost two relatives to malaria and TB in India. You had a lucky escape. Look, and I will be honest with you,

I was feeling depressed for a while … I won't go into details now, but I was on medication. There is no harm in admitting that you need help."

"Oh no, Molly. My mind has been so occupied with what happened to me that I haven't thought of you. I am sorry. I know so little about your life here."

"I couldn't write to you about everything, you know. I had some issues. Thankfully, they're all in the past. And now, I see you like this. It's breaking my heart."

"Sorry. I will get myself together." Grace wiped her wet nose.

"I know, James has his issues, but he's trying his best to help you. You both lost your child. It's a very traumatic experience. Now is not the time to talk about divorce. When you get on your feet you will decide what to do, but for now, you need help."

"Molly. Thanks a lot for your support. You are such a treasure, always there for me." They hugged each other again.

Over the next few months Grace saw Molly less and less. She couldn't understand why. And she felt strange. Sometimes she had a clear mind and even managed to go out to the garden, but sometimes her mind was a blur. She had headaches and lost her appetite. James was constantly around her. She was puzzled.

Why did he insist on being affectionate? He was always sitting near her, always holding her hand, insisting that he didn't want to lose her and that he would do everything to make her feel better. The only power she had was to not show any reaction to his attention. Every time he did something affectionate, she made sure to turn her head away. One day James said that he couldn't tolerate such behaviour from his wife anymore.

"You don't need to; you know what to do." For once Grace's mind was clear enough to make the brave move to tell him what she wanted. "Please let me go!"

"Let you go? Are you out of your mind? I'm not going to leave my wife in such a state."

"I'm fine."

"You are not fine and I arranged for you to see a doctor."

"A doctor? Again?"

"You have some health issues, my darling. Probably psychological issues. You are not eating well, not talking to me and constantly snapping at me. You need medical treatment. I want you to get well."

"Why would you say such a thing? Psychological issues? I'm absolutely fine. I don't have any issues. I'm just grieving for my child."

"*Our* child."

Grace looked at him, even though she didn't want to, but she needed to see his eyes. He glared at her without blinking, his anger rising, and he shouted, "*Our* child! I have done everything I could. You have been depressed from the day we came back to England. I even put aside my own business and tried my best to help you. I have been here day and night at your side, but you keep pushing me away. It can't go on like this."

He pulled a piece of paper from the internal pocket of his jacket and held it in front of Grace.

"Look at this. Read it. Read it again. I showed it to you before, but you didn't believe me."

She took it slowly and started to read. It was the death certificate of her son. It looked real and had an official stamp. He quickly took it back from her and returned it to his pocket.

Then he turned and said in a much softer voice, "Darling, we are both stressed. I know you are grieving. So am I. I do everything for you, you know that. Please, just see the doctor and then tell me what you want to do." He looked at Grace with begging yet empty eyes. "Agreed?"

Grace met his eyes briefly, then moved her gaze to the window. She knew he wouldn't allow her to do anything until she agreed with him on something at least. And what if she had the chance to ask for help when she saw the doctor?

"Fine," was her short answer.

Grace didn't realise that the doctor would be coming to see her, not the other way around. James was in the room all the time while the doctor spoke with her, so there was no way she could ask the doctor anything.

What made things worse was that she overheard the doctor telling James, "Mrs Clifford is suffering from a mix of anxiety and depression. Many mothers who lose their child experience the same. It takes time, but it can be cured."

"Will she be back to normal?"

"Yes, of course, she will. Mrs Clifford just needs some rest and medication. I will give you a prescription for your wife." The doctor wrote something on a piece of paper, turning his back to Grace, and then gave it to James. "I will visit Mrs Clifford in a month's time, the dose …"

"Let's discuss it outside, if you don't mind. My wife needs rest." James almost pushed the doctor to the door. Grace was too weak to ask for anything or argue with her husband. She closed her eyes when the door shut behind them. She felt suspicious of James. *What is he up to?*

White Cliffs 1948

Suspicious thoughts

The fresh sea breeze touched Grace's face. She loved the smell of salt and seaweed. She took a deep breath. It was early spring, full of chilly air and biting wind, but Grace enjoyed sitting in the garden with a woolly blanket around her legs. She recalled Molly's visit and their conversation a month after she moved back to White Cliffs.

"Molly, please tell me what you know. He didn't tell me anything. Why did he suddenly agree for me to return to White Cliffs?"

"Grace, I'm so glad to see you are doing well. Do you really want to know the details? How will it help you? You're here, in your home, and he's in London. Maybe it's best not to open healing wounds."

"I couldn't do that, you know. I keep thinking about it. I couldn't."

"I know."

"No matter what he said, I couldn't do that."

"I believe it was an accident, Grace. I know you wouldn't do that."

"But why did he say that I wanted to kill myself?"

"I don't know. He just called Oliver and me that day to tell us that you had attempted suicide. It was very disturbing, but, of course, we didn't believe it. Sorry I stopped coming to see you. That month was tough for our family too. James also kept saying that you were asleep or couldn't be disturbed."

"It's fine, Molly, I don't blame you. I know he prevented anybody from seeing me. That was another example of his suspicious behaviour."

"I managed to speak to the hospital doctor who saw you when you were first admitted. It was later on that your family doctor took over."

"James didn't mention another doctor."

"Of course, he wouldn't mention him. The doctor told me that you took lots of sedative pills, but he couldn't find a prescription for them. Also, he said that you were taking medication to treat your depression for too long. So, taking the two medications together and their side effects had an unfortunate impact on you. Do you remember taking all those pills at the same time?"

"No, I don't, but I can't tell you for sure. James was giving me tablets every morning and evening. The same tablets. Some of them were coloured."

"James, of course, didn't explain anything in detail to me or Oliver. I was shocked Grace. I couldn't figure out what had happened to you."

"I couldn't do that, Molly, I couldn't. I know for sure!"

"Don't worry about it now, Grace. All of this is in the past. It was an accident. You were under the effect of strong medication. I told James that I spoke to the doctor, and I asked him about the sedative pills. His face went white. James said they were his. But he didn't like me questioning him. So, I told him what I thought of him."

"Did you?"

"I did." Molly smiled. "I was so angry with him. When Oliver went to visit his father and you were sleeping in bed after James brought you home from hospital, I unleased all my anger on him. I told him he was a selfish and unworthy husband. I told him that if he wouldn't allow you to move back to White Cliffs, I would make a lot of noise about your medication and how you were treated by him."

"Goodness, Molly! You were so brave. You have changed a lot, you know. You did something I couldn't do."

"Oh, Grace, you never know how you will react when life presses you to the ground, face down. After our first meeting on your return, I thought about what you said a lot. I could tell something was wrong and that you were not able to do anything about it on your own. I didn't care what James thought of me after that, so I said what was on my mind."

"Molly, I owe you, my life. If you hadn't taken me out of that prison, I don't know what would have happened to me."

"Honestly, I don't think he wanted to harm you deliberately. I'm not defending him, no! But something was there on his face when I questioned him. He was … scared."

"James, scared? I don't believe it."

"He said he would never harm you. He just didn't know what to do. I actually think he loves you, Grace."

"James? Oh, please, Molly."

"You know sometimes love can turn into an obsession."

"It's more like he wanted to possess me. How I could have trusted him with giving me medication, I don't know. I didn't even check what I was taking. Silly me."

"James is obsessed with you. He is afraid to lose you. He wanted to keep you at home. Being under medication, you were the way he liked you to be, not demanding or telling him that you would leave him. I think that's what happened. And when you were on medication for too long, you started to get confused. It could have happened to anybody, Grace, not just to you. It's not your fault. I know you wouldn't do that."

"Thank you, Molly."

"Grace, please don't think about it anymore. You got what you wanted. You are separated. He won't bother you any longer. I think he has reverted to his bad habits and is busy with his life in London anyway."

After they had tea, Molly surprised Grace with her personal news.

"Sorry, I couldn't speak to you earlier. You needed time to get well, and I didn't know how to tell you."

"You can always tell me anything, Molly, any time. I can see by looking at you, you have some news. Am I right?"

"Yes. Oliver and I are expecting our first baby. Finally!"

"Oh, Molly. That's amazing!" Grace exclaimed, getting up from her chair to give Molly a big hug. "Congratulations, sweetheart. Congratulations. That's wonderful news." Then Grace put her hands on Molly's shoulders and looked her up and down. "I thought you had just put on some weight." They both laughed.

"Thank you, Grace. I just thought … you lost your child recently and needed time to heal, but at the same time I knew I wouldn't be able to hide it for too long."

"That's very considerate of you, thanks, Molly, but you did the right thing telling me. I'm so happy for you. It has made my day. How far gone are you?"

"Almost five months, now."

"You are hiding it very well, I have to say. Are you eating at all? You know they say you have to eat for two. I can't believe you are almost five months pregnant. You haven't an ounce on you." They laughed again.

Grace pulled up her woolly blanket and smiled, remembering that meeting with Molly. It was a few months back. Molly had visited Grace a few more times and then stopped. Her belly had grown quickly after that and she didn't want to be on the road for too long. Molly and Oliver lived at the Clifford Estate in York; Grace understood it was too far from there to the south of England, so she was just patiently waiting for her friend to be able to visit her again.

Grace had returned to her artwork and it was slowly healing her. She was reading a lot and spent much of her time gardening. She was sad that almost all her grandmother's horses were gone; only two old mares were left in the stables. She was afraid to ride them, so she just looked after them. Her grandmother had loved horses, but Grace wasn't able to continue what Elizabeth had done. James hadn't been interested in the horse business at all. He had taken her to India straight away and left his lawyer to handle everything related to the Bellmore Estate. She later learned that he had spent almost all the money the business had earned. So, when she moved back to White Cliffs it was on the condition that she would take care of her grandmother's estate herself. James agreed as long as she postponed the divorce. The Bellmore Estate's only remaining income was from leasing out the land. Elizabeth had always been a cautious person. She told Grace that the land was the best way to preserve income and, in spite of offers from many farmers wanting to buy it off her, Elizabeth had never sold it. Now it could provide Grace with a living.

Charlotte

New life and hope

One sunny summer day in 1948, Grace was sitting in the drawing room of White Cliffs. She was looking out the window, turning her face to the sun, when she saw Oliver's car make its way up the driveway. Though the visit was planned, she was suddenly beset by nerves because she knew that the car didn't only contain Oliver and Molly, it also contained their two-month-old baby daughter, Charlotte. Grace sat in the armchair by the window and listened to the sound of Molly's footsteps on the gravel, the doorbell ringing, and the butler ushering her guests in.

When Molly entered the drawing room, Grace froze for a moment, waiting eagerly to see Charlotte.

"Hello, Grace."

"How are you, Grace?" asked Oliver.

"Hello, you two. So wonderful to see you both again. Ah, sorry, there are three of you now." Soft happy smiles spread on their faces. "Thank you for coming. Please come in, come in."

"We finally made it." Molly looked down at her daughter

and moved a blanket away from Charlotte's face. "Charlotte was sleeping all the way, but she has now started to move. Maybe she is hungry. I will feed her soon. I'm sure you want to see her first."

When Grace saw Molly holding Charlotte, it reminded her of India and that house in the mountains. The bed with sweaty sheets covered in blood and … her baby who had disappeared afterwards; she had never had a chance to hold her own baby. It was a strange moment full of sadness and happiness at the same time as she stared at the bundle in Molly's arms. Her friend started to walk towards Grace, then stopped when a noise in the blanket caught their attention. Charlotte had started to cry. When Grace heard her, she immediately rushed to Molly.

"Can I hold her?"

"Of course, Grace. Please do."

When Grace took Charlotte in her arms for the first time, they bonded straight away. The baby stopped crying and smiled at her, amusing everybody. For the rest of the day Grace walked with the baby in her arms, looking admiringly at her. She couldn't take her eyes off Charlotte.

A tray with tea was brought in by the butler who glanced over with a wry smile. Oliver stretched out his arms and offered to take Charlotte off Grace's hands while she and Molly drank tea. The day was coming to an end. The light of the setting sun was streaming through the window and a gentle breeze moved the curtains. Grace felt at ease but kept constantly peeping over at Charlotte. She couldn't wait to take her back from Oliver.

"She never stops smiling at you," said Molly jealously, when Grace took Charlotte back in her arms.

"She's a gorgeous girl. Look at her. Look, Molly."

"Your arms must be tired, Grace. You have been holding her all day."

"Not at all, Molly. She is such a tiny, beautiful thing." Grace turned to Oliver who was sitting on the sofa with a newspaper in his hands. "Oliver, you must be over the moon, proud father."

"You said it, Grace. I am. I guess we don't have to hire a nanny. We have one already." He winked at Molly.

Molly stayed with Grace for a few days while Oliver went to London to see his father. But it wasn't enough for Grace. She asked her friend to come back with Charlotte as often as she could. Molly and Oliver asked Grace to become Charlotte's godmother and she accepted with joy and pride. The relationship between Grace and Molly blossomed, their love and care for each other growing stronger day by day. They loved Charlotte equally; it was as if she had two mothers. In the months that followed, Molly spent many of her days at White Cliffs. She had to move in there because the Clifford Estate needed serious renovations. The roof was leaking, chimneys were blocked and the plumbing needed urgent attention. The work made a lot of noise, which wasn't good for either the baby or Molly. Grace was delighted to have them at White Cliffs. Molly was happy also. It helped, she said, to share the duties of motherhood with her friend, and to have someone to talk to, someone who understood her. Soon, it became the norm for Oliver to join them and spend weekends there, and for them to all dine together.

It was late autumn, a stormy evening with lots of rain. The three of them were at the dining table when the phone rang. Grace jerked in her seat.

"Doesn't it sound sharper than usual?"

They listened to the butler answering the phone, which was in the hall. Then they heard his footsteps coming closer to the dining room.

"A call for you, Mr Clifford," he said, gesturing politely at Oliver.

Oliver walked briskly to the phone. It wasn't possible to hear what he said, but it seemed from the way he held the phone, and at one point looked back towards Molly, that something must be wrong.

"What is it?" Molly called out to him.

Grace looked at Molly, worried. When Oliver walked back in, his wife ran to him.

"That was my father on the phone," he said. "He is not well

and is afraid to stay at the house on his own. His voice was trembling."

"What's wrong, Oliver?" Molly wanted him to tell her everything.

Oliver whispered in his wife's ear, but Grace overheard him. "James has just phoned my father and said that he's coming over. He sounded drunk and angry."

"He hasn't been there for years. What does he want from his father?" Molly wondered.

"He didn't explain the reason for his visit. He just said that he is coming to get the truth out of him."

Grace was tense, watching Oliver and Molly discussing what to do. They agreed they should travel to London immediately. Oliver said that his father shouldn't live on his own at his London residence, but it was Lord Clifford's decision.

"Can't you stay until tomorrow?" said Grace anxiously. She didn't know why, but the thought of them driving away that very evening filled her with foreboding.

"I'm afraid I can't," said Oliver. "The weather is very bad. I would prefer Molly and Charlotte to stay with you, Grace."

"I'm going with you!" said Molly. "No way will I let you go on your own. I might be able to help. James is more likely to behave himself in front of his sister-in-law."

Oliver silently agreed with his wife and turned to Grace. "Grace, may I bring my father here until he's feeling better?

As you know, our house in York is under renovation. He has always loved White Cliffs and found it restful here."

"Of course, Oliver. His Lordship can stay here as long as he likes. He is my father-in-law after all. The doors of White Cliffs are always open for him. In the meantime, why don't you leave Charlotte with me?"

They agreed that Charlotte would stay with Grace and they, with Lord Clifford, would come back to White Cliffs the next day.

Before Molly and Oliver got into the car, Grace went upstairs to get Charlotte and when she watched Molly, lovingly holding and kissing her daughter, Grace's heart sank.

"I don't like it," she said hugging Molly. "I don't like it. Please stay. Maybe you could change your mind?"

"I confess that I don't really want to go and leave my little angel behind. It's the first time I will be separated from my daughter. But I can't let Oliver go on his own. His relationship with James is not really the way it was. They don't often speak to each other anymore. When you left him, Grace, he became antagonistic, even with Oliver. That's what makes me worry if just Oliver goes there."

"I see and understand. Please don't worry about Charlotte. I will look after her, and you are coming back tomorrow. So, it's just one night. Please be careful and drive safely."

"I will phone you first thing in the morning," said Molly.

"Oliver is a good driver. We will be fine."

Grace hugged her friend. But her fears weren't allayed. As the car pulled away, she held Charlotte tight and waved goodbye. From where she stood, it seemed as though Molly was crying through her smile.

Thick fog had begun to descend quickly.

A tragic day

The blows of fate

Grace was playing with Charlotte in the drawing room when a car drove up the driveway. She rushed to the window. It wasn't Oliver's car and it was moving slowly. It was midday and Grace had been up since dawn, after a sleepless night, partly because Charlotte had cried a lot, which was unusual for her, and partly because Grace had been so worried. She had spent the morning trying to amuse the baby and kept staring at the clock and then the phone. Why had Molly not called yet? And why had no one answered when she had called Lord Clifford's?

Grace watched as the car stopped. It was a Wolseley police car. A man got out of it, and the butler went outside and began talking to him. Her heart pounded. Without thinking, she lifted Charlotte into her arms and followed the butler out of the door.

"This is Constable Jones," said the butler.

"Mrs Clifford?"

"Yes?"

"Could we please talk? Maybe inside?"

"Of course, come in." Grace led the constable into the drawing room.

"I don't know where to start."

"Please." Grace gestured at an armchair and the two of them sat, opposite each other. The constable fiddled with his cap.

"I'm sorry to tell you this, Mrs Clifford," he began. "There was a fire in your father-in-law's house last night."

Grace covered her mouth with her hand.

"Was Lord Clifford hurt? Who else was in the house? His son Oliver and his wife went there yesterday. Have you seen them?"

"Mr Clifford and his wife … they didn't make it there," he replied quietly, almost whispering.

"What do you mean they didn't make it there? Where are they?"

"They …" The constable took a breath. "They were involved in a car accident last night and sadly … neither of them survived."

"No!" Grace screamed. "No. They said they had to be back today. Do you have any further information? What hospital are they in? I want to see them."

She clutched the chair so hard, her knuckles turned white. Charlotte, whom she was still holding in her other arm, began to cry. Grace stood and started to pace the room, trying to calm the crying baby.

"That's not all," the constable continued. "I'm afraid I have other sad news. Please forgive me, but I have to tell you. Your father-in-law … died after an hour or so after he was brought to hospital. Unfortunately, he couldn't be saved. Your husband, Mr Clifford … was badly injured, but, fortunately, he is alive. I'm sorry to bring you such terrible news, Mrs Clifford. Your father-in-law's lawyer will contact you. I'm so sorry, Mrs Clifford." With his head down, the constable left her.

Later that day everyone in the house learned from the newspapers that Molly and Oliver had died in a car accident after a large truck crashed into them.

'… It would have been hard to see anything in the pouring rain so late at night. Both driver and passenger died instantly …'

The same newspapers were also full of headlines about the fire in Lord Clifford's London house. The world had turned upside down for Grace again. Numb with shock, she lay in bed, holding Charlotte next to her and the lock of her son's hair in her hand. She was lost, alone and scared.

Grace was broken after the funeral and the many hours of talking to her father-in-law and husband's lawyers. She was overwhelmed with the deluge of papers, documents and information she didn't understand that had suddenly been dumped on her. She didn't have time for James and didn't want to visit him in the hospital. But eventually, following her lawyer's advice, she did.

When she arrived, he was asleep. At least she didn't have to talk to him. Standing there, she noticed, without any emotion, that half of his face had been badly burned. The doctor said he might not be able to see in one eye and the nerves on his right leg were badly damaged. He was going to have to undergo multiple operations and would have a long rehabilitation. He probably wouldn't walk again.

Grace stayed in the hospital room silently for a few minutes digesting what the doctor told her. She looked at James again. The fact that he would only be able to partially see in future and couldn't walk didn't bother her. *He could have done me the favour of dying himself*, she told herself bitterly. He looked miserable, but she didn't feel anything towards him. She didn't even think of him as her husband anymore. They hadn't seen each other for over a year. He had tried to phone her, but she wouldn't speak with him. If James had not visited his father that evening, Molly, Oliver and Lord Clifford would still be alive.

Grace wanted to find out exactly what had happened that night. She asked Lord Clifford's butler to meet her in the park. He agreed. When she left the hospital, she went straight there. What she learned from the butler shocked her even more. He told her that James was very drunk that night and could barely stand straight on his feet when he arrived. Lord Clifford was in his study downstairs. He actually found a key and had wanted to lock himself in there to prevent James getting in, but the butler admitted that it was his advice not to do so, because he was afraid if something happened to Lord Clifford, he wouldn't be able to help. When James got inside his father's study, he closed and locked the door behind him. All the butler could hear was James shouting at his father. There was a lot said about James's mother; James blamed his father for her death. He accused him of everything that was wrong in his life. That Lord Clifford had always loved Oliver more than him and now wanted to leave everything to Oliver. He mentioned his father's Will. Then the butler had heard Lord Clifford calling out for him.

"I tried to open the door, but it was locked from the inside. I tried to help, Mrs Clifford. I tried." The butler swiped his arm across his nose. "I think something got into the fire. I blame myself; I lit the fire that evening. I wanted to warm up the room for Lord Clifford. He had just come back from hospital and looked fragile in his last days. I smelled the smoke, but I couldn't hear Lord Clifford's voice anymore. Only James screaming 'where is that damn key'. I think he lost the key and couldn't open the door. So, I went to the basement to find a second key, but I couldn't find it."

Grace could tell the butler was almost crying. She gently placed her hand on his upper arm in support, but she didn't interrupt him.

"When I came back, there was a lot of smoke. I called the fire brigade and the hospital, the emergency department. I was worried for Lord Clifford. He had stopped calling for me. And James. I didn't hear him either. It was bad, Mrs Clifford. It felt terrible. The fire was everywhere. I ran outside, fell on the ground and prayed."

Grace thanked the butler and let him go. He was very upset. She didn't want to keep him there for longer. She had got enough information to understand what happened. What else did she need to know about her husband to hate him more than she already did? Grace didn't like to get angry. She had learned to keep her emotions at the right level, but she couldn't help herself in that moment.

Her thoughts were all about Charlotte. Grace understood that, more than ever, she needed to be strong for this baby who was only six months old. She herself, accustomed to the blows of fate, could survive the next trial, but for Charlotte, life would be difficult without her mother. Putting her to bed that night, she sat by the cot.

"I promise to do everything for you and will always be by your side, my little angel," she whispered. It was hard for her. Every time she looked at Charlotte, she saw Molly. She missed Molly immensely. She had lost all of them, her family, her friends. During the day, when she was with Charlotte, whatever she was doing, she would stay calm, but she couldn't hide her feelings at night. She cried a lot. She was afraid for both of their futures, her own and Charlotte's.

The day arrived to meet with the lawyers to arrange custody of Molly and Oliver's daughter.

The decision

Beyond the pale

Lord Clifford had bequeathed everything to his granddaughter, Charlotte, via a trust that she could access once she turned twenty-one. James was so angry when he learned that his father, unbeknown to anyone, had made a new Will. In it he had, at least, left James something; that something being the house James had inadvertently set fire to on that fateful night.

Molly and Oliver had also managed to make a Will, which stipulated that, in the event of their death, Grace and James were to become Charlotte's guardians. Their entire fortune passed to their daughter as well, with the guardians allowed to use some of it for her education and other costs associated with raising her. Grace and James had been given equal rights, which meant they were to make all decisions concerning Charlotte together. Not only that, but Grace found herself obliged to take care of her husband as well, because raising Charlotte with him meant they had to live together. It was unbelievably hard for her to accept. Grace prayed for the strength to endure it all. This was another test of fate. For the sake of Charlotte and in memory of Molly, she would accept this test. So, she signed all the necessary papers and prepared the house for James's return from the hospital.

The first few months were the most difficult. James writhed in pain, and his rehabilitation was slow. He was in agony. Yet, as soon as he could, he signed the paperwork to adopt Charlotte. He didn't have a choice. Grace knew that he would do anything to stay with her. Especially now that they were to live under the same roof for Charlotte's sake. He agreed with her on almost everything. They decided to live in James's house in London because he needed constant medical treatments.

The consolation for Grace was the large garden at the back of the house, where she could be alone with Charlotte. Its fence was lined with tall trees and shrubs that hid the house from the road. The garden needed some work but wasn't in too bad a state. In other words, it was a project she could take on. There was a carved wooden gazebo, a bench in the corner and some flowers. She discovered the house had a back door which led straight to the stairs on the first floor where Charlotte's and her rooms were; this allowed her to leave and return without James seeing her. The ground floor was James's and he didn't allow anything to be changed there.

Charlotte grew up loved and cared for. She called Grace

'Mummy', but she didn't call James by any name, except on rare occasions if she were thanking him for something or wishing him happy birthday, when she would call him 'James'. When Charlotte was five years old, Grace told her about her parents. Charlotte, in spite of her youth, accepted this information calmly. She asked Grace a few questions, stared at the photo of her parents for a long time, and then she went up to Grace and hugged her tightly. After that conversation, she stayed in her room all day. But the following morning, it was as if nothing had happened; Charlotte came down to breakfast and called her 'Mummy', as she always did. Grace kissed her daughter on the cheek and smoothed a lock of Charlotte's hair down over her face. Mother and daughter smiled at each other.

Charlotte was growing up to be a smart girl. She noticed the tension between Grace and James. She didn't ask questions, but she didn't like it and, though she was respectful towards James, it was clear her feelings for him were cold. Every holiday and on many weekends through the years, Grace and Charlotte went to White Cliffs. They both enjoyed their time and privacy there.

When Charlotte graduated from private school, Grace told her about her inheritance. Charlotte didn't show much interest at that time. She was preoccupied by her studies as she prepared for university. It was only when Charlotte started university that Grace returned to White Cliffs permanently, leaving

James alone at his house. She was forty-four years old and James was sixty-two. By then, James was in his bedroom most of the time. He could no longer move around the house on his own even in his wheelchair. His eyesight had deteriorated; he could hardly see. He couldn't prevent Grace from leaving him.

A letter from the past

Shocking secrets, May 1969

Three years later, still shaken by her earlier nightmare, Grace remained in the peaceful surroundings of the garden at White Cliffs. She sat under the protective shelter of the hawthorn tree which she had planted with her grandmother, Elizabeth, almost forty years ago. It blossomed with pinkish white flowers. Her grandmother once told her that in Ireland, some people feared the hawthorn because of a legend that dead people were often buried under them and the smell from the trees attracted bad luck and more death. Other people treasured the hawthorn like a holy tree and never cut it down, even when it grew in the middle of a field, because fairies lived under them. Many people had hawthorn trees in their gardens and believed they would protect their homes and families, and would bring good luck. Grace was one of the people who believed in the goodness of the hawthorn. Through the tree, she felt a connection with her mother. She spent a lot of her time on the wooden bench under the shade of its lush crown.

From the pocket of her dressing gown she took out a small

framed photograph which she had taken on impulse from her chest of drawers on the way to the garden. In it, her mother was standing next to a hawthorn tree with the infant Grace in her arms. Grace looked at the back of the photograph, upon which her mother's words were written:

May this hawthorn protect my little Grace.

Over the twenty-two years since Grace had returned to England from India, she had done many things to alleviate her suffering. She found the strength to keep going. She meditated every day and resumed her art work, especially in the countryside, which provided her with excellent subject matter. Grace did a lot of gardening as well, which she found was very healing. All these things had helped. She forgave herself for past mistakes, for not doing things she ought to have done. She also forgave others. But lately, memories from the past had started flooding through her like an overflowing river. And now, the nightmare was back.

Grace sat there in her deep thoughts until her housekeeper arrived and passed her a letter that she said had just been delivered. She hesitated to open the letter at first because she didn't recognise the lawyer's name on the back of the envelope, although she knew the firm name and address. It was from Lord Clifford's lawyers. She opened the envelope with curiosity. There was a letter and another envelope inside. The first letter was from the new lawyer for the Clifford family. He said that he had enclosed an envelope addressed to Grace Clifford. It seemed that this envelope had been lost in the files and had only recently been discovered when he started in his new position, after the previous lawyer died. The new lawyer apologised for the twenty-one year delay in sending the letter to her but explained that it was his duty to do so now. It was from her longdeceased father-in-law.

Grace turned over the envelope in her hands. Its glue was long yellowed, yet it was still sealed. No living person knew its contents. Recollecting her life until now, she wasn't ready for another surprise. She opened the envelope. It contained a letter and a photograph. She was calm. The sun's rays touched her hand, then moved slowly onto the letter. She started to read.

Dear Grace,

I expect you will be surprised to receive this letter from me, and even more surprised to read its contents. If you are reading this letter, it means I am gone. I did not have the courage to tell you this when I was alive. After you and James came back from India and I received the news of you losing your child at birth, I realised that James had not told you the truth. Your wellbeing concerned me, so I decided to write to you instead of talking to you; I just did not want to give you more grief at that time.

But first there is something else that I must start with. I am not James's father and he does not know about this. In short, my wife had an affair with an English engineer called Thomas Howard in India. I never told my wife that I discovered her affair or the ruby ring that was given to her by Thomas. James was the product of that affair. I loved her and raised James as my son. As you already know, we did not have a good relationship, but I tried my best. In the photograph enclosed with this letter you will see Thomas Howard, James's father. I found this photograph in my wife's things after she died.

Grace stopped reading for a moment and looked at the photograph, admitting straight away that James had got a lot of his looks from Thomas. She was shocked, but she wanted to finish reading the letter. She placed the photograph on the bench next to her and continued to read.

Now, about James.

James could not have children, Grace. Your child was not his son and James knew it.

Many scenes from her life crossed her mind in seconds. When and how James had proposed to her. What she had overheard that day at the Clifford Estate when James had told his father not to tell her something. How James had been disrespectful to her and hurt her so much. That night on the plantations and what happened afterwards. James's strangely loving attitude to her during her pregnancy. The day of her son's birth. James showing her the death certificate. James claiming he was the father! He had actually done everything he could to convince her that he was the father. And he had succeeded. But deep inside, she'd always had doubts. Always. It had disturbed her greatly through the years. She couldn't say what it was, but she always felt that there was something hidden from her. Her heart was crying and screaming for the truth. Now, she had it in her hands, in this old, faded letter.

That line was the hardest part of the letter to digest, her brain, at first, was refusing to process it. She read it many times before she started to breathe again. The letter continued.

> As a result of a childhood illness, James became infertile. When he learned he would not have children, his character changed and he became more aggressive and angrier. He started to drink and womanise a lot. I suggested to him on your engagement day that it was only fair he told you about it, but he reacted badly.
>
> I can no longer carry these secrets. I beg for your forgiveness, Grace. I am sorry.
>
> Lord Clifford.

Now Grace understood why James was angry towards her on their wedding night, when he had lost his temper for the first time, and then the many times after that. His silence made her suffer. She would have understood if he had told her that he couldn't have children, but he never did. Grace pressed her hand on her forehead as she kicked herself. James *knew* that the child wasn't his child. Why did he tell her that the baby they lost was his son? What was that lie for?

A pain pierced through Grace's body from her head to her feet. Her heart began to race. She repeated to herself again and again, *James isn't the father of my son.*

The information in the letter shocked Grace to the core. She had unwillingly stumbled onto disturbing secrets. She took a moment to catch her breath. Her thoughts were chasing each other endlessly. The real father of her child was … Aadir. She had not heard from him since that night. He hadn't tried to find her and that upset Grace greatly. But she still remembered his last kiss. Grace touched her lips with her fingers and closed her eyes. Then happy feelings overcame her pain. Tears slowly began pouring down her cheeks, but when they reached her lips, she smiled. Salty drops got into her mouth. She swallowed them and turned her face to the sun, repeating in her head, *Aadir. Aadir. The father of my child ... Aadir!*

She was grateful for the fact that the truth had eventually come out. Yes, it was too late … or maybe not too late? She opened her eyes. *My son*, she said to herself. *I need to know where you are, dead or alive. I need to know!*

That evening Charlotte came back home from London where she had been spending some time with her friends after graduation. Her mother's pale skin frightened her, but Grace assured her daughter that everything was fine. Just a sleepless night, that was all. After they had tea together by the fire, their usual evening ritual, Grace suddenly turned to Charlotte and asked, “Would you like to go to India?”

One last thing

Unleashed rage

The front door opened, and Grace rushed inside of James's house like a gale blowing through an open window. She had lived there for many years raising Charlotte but had never accepted that house as her home. Without stopping, she said to the butler, dismissively waving her hand in the air, "Don't bother closing the door. I'm not staying for long."

Grace found James in the drawing room, sitting in his wheelchair by the window. The first thought that came to her mind was to give him a big slap. She stopped at the door and put her hand to her chest, catching her breath. She couldn't find it in herself to slap her husband, even if he was a cheater, an abuser and a liar. His head was tilted to one side and downwards, with his one good eye closed. He was probably sleeping and looked wretched. She glanced over to the table on the left of the room and noticed a crystal decanter of whiskey and a glass of water next to it. Grace was by the table in a second. Her hand, moving towards the glass of water, suddenly shifted in the opposite direction. She poured herself a half glass of whiskey and knocked it back at once. The golden, caramel liquid burned her throat and cascaded down into her stomach. She winced and bit her lower lip. It was her first experience of strong alcohol. Then she quickly returned to her place by the door. She didn't want to wait for the warmth of the whiskey to begin to relax her. While it burned her throat it gave her the strength to resist her husband.

"Grace?" James stared at her like she was a ghost.

Of course, he would be surprised because he hadn't seen her for three years. When she left the last time, she had said that she would never come back to this house.

"I'm glad to see you, Grace. Please come in, don't stand at the door."

"How could you do this to me? How *could* you?" Grace shouted at James and took a few steps towards him. The whiskey gave her Dutch courage. She had never been this angry before and she watched as James's face froze. She, herself, hadn't known that she could experience such rage.

"What do you mean, darling?"

She stared at him. "You knew! You knew all these years. Why? Why did you keep it from me?" She didn't want to come too close to him and instead just stared at him. With that one eye, he looked at her in amusement and … fear.

"Grace, I don't know what you are talking about."

"Really? You really don't know? The doctor told me that you would lose an eye, but not your memory."

"Grace, what happened to you? I have never seen you like *this* before."

"What happened to me? How dare you ask me that question. Have you already forgotten *what* you did to me? What you hid from me?" Memories immediately tightened her chest, but she swallowed the unwanted urge to cry.

"What did I hide?"

She was startled by his arrogance and obstinacy. "I hate you right now! I hate you with all my heart."

"Grace … whatever it is … I'm still glad to see you. Please sit down and we can talk." James tried to move his wheelchair towards her.

Grace put her hand out in front of her, signalling that he should stay where he was and not come closer. She tried to calm down. Anger was building inside her like a volcano about to erupt, preventing her from thinking straight. Was she angry just with James, or with herself as well for allowing him to manipulate and hurt her for so many years? She had grieved for too long and prevented herself from facing the truth and understanding what she had been dragged into. She walked to the window and looked out, taking a deep breath.

"I found out that you can't have children."

"How … did you … find out?" James stuttered.

"It doesn't matter. You lied to me!"

"I didn't lie … just didn't tell you … *I* didn't believe it anyway."

"How could you say the child I lost was *your* son? How could you claim that?" She looked at his face with such intensity, it pierced right through him.

James didn't say anything, turning his head away.

"I would have understood if you had told me."

"Would you? All I wanted, Grace ..."

"So, you knew that you weren't the father of my child when you took me away from Darjeeling. Did you have a plan before you took me away? Why did you play the caring and loving husband during my pregnancy then?"

"You have a lot of questions for me today. Have you ever thought that perhaps I am not that bad, after all?"

"You are not that bad, you're right. You are much worse. I can't even find words to describe you. You are a despicable man."

"I wanted us to be a family. I thought ... I hoped that the child could be mine. I wanted ..." He started to cough.

Grace looked at the glass of water on the table and went to get it for him. While he was drinking water, she thought to herself, *what if he really hoped and believed that the child was his?* She just realised that James lived with a glimmer of hope that he could have a child. It wasn't her place to take away his hope, even if he took hers away. He wanted a family. There was nothing wrong with that, even when he was told he couldn't have children. The problem was that he didn't want to share his hope and dreams with *her.* What he had done to her and how he treated her in India was intolerable. The memory of the past was too uncomfortable for her and awoke the trauma she tried to heal for all these years. When he finished drinking the water, she took it away from him. Knowing her husband and his habit of breaking glasses, it was better to remove it.

"You wanted us to be a family? Why take me to England without giving me the chance to say goodbye to my son? Why keep me drugged and almost lifeless under that medication in your house like a prisoner? What kind of family were you dreaming of?"

"I was afraid to lose you. All I wanted was … to be with you."

"By force? You thought you could keep me next to you by force and then what? You knew that were it not for Charlotte I wanted to divorce you … But why did you still hide the truth?"

"I did what I did, but what about you? Are you admitting that you had an affair with that Indian savage? What about your marriage vows to me?" His gaze was darting from left to right, but he couldn't get up. He touched the burned side of his face and looked around the room like he was searching for someone to help him. He was helpless and he had finally said it. He had accused her of adultery.

Grace clenched her teeth when she heard *what* he called Aadir. So, James knew about her and Aadir, but he had been silent for twenty-two years. *Another secret!* His accusations couldn't touch her, but why *now*? The insane urge to say something that would hurt him rushed like a hurricane inside her. She immediately wanted to tell him that he himself was a child born from an affair. But with incredible willpower, she let her brain take control over her broken heart and she paused instead, breathing through the enormous amount of fury she felt.

"Marriage? Our marriage was a sham. You deceived me into getting married to you. You hypocrite! Many times, you were constantly doing the very thing you are now accusing me of. You could have just divorced me when you found out about it."

"Did you love me, Grace?"

His question threw her. She wasn't expecting it. She wanted him to suffer like he had made her suffer.

"What do *you* think?"

She looked at his burned skin and imagined the fire, and him being inside it, the same fire that was in her nightmares. He held her gaze; that begging question in his eye. Did she love him? He looked like he wanted to scream because he felt so helpless. He couldn't get to her and hurt her anymore. She knew he was feeling useless and worthless at that moment as he begged for her love. He knew she had stopped loving him a long time ago and now seemed to be hoping to live in the past because his present life was hurting him too much.

She wanted to tell him that she had actually loved him only once: that night at the gate lodge. Their first night. After that, it was just a chain of events she was forced into. The decisions were made for her. The choices were limited. Her life wasn't in her hands. Her trust had been tested and was broken. She had been abused by him and he had lied to her so many times and now he was asking if she *loved* him. He had almost succeeded in distracting her from the reason she was there. But it was not his or her pain, her anger, or even discovering the secret of who the father of her child was that had brought Grace to face James again. What she did next, surprised even her. She moved closer to him, placed her hands on the wheelchair's arms and looked into his one eye, her gaze piercing his like a knife.

"Is my son *alive* and where is he?"

James didn't blink, holding her gaze, but his eye darted around, its depths not changed, still as empty as always. A few drops of sweat appeared on his forehead.

Suddenly, with a hint of a smile on his lips, he blurted out at her, "Do I smell whiskey, darling? So … we have more in common that we thought."

Grace stood straight and took a few steps back from him. Showing no reaction to his provocative comment, she changed her tone, calmer this time.

"I will ask you one more time. Where is my son?"

James got a handkerchief from his pocket and wiped away his sweat. After a short pause, he murmured with bitterness, "I *told* you where …"

Grace was screaming inside with frustration, but she realised that she wouldn't get the answer she was seeking from the pathetic excuse of a man in front of her. His stubborn heart refused to relent. She crossed the room and placed her wedding ring on the table. She didn't know why she had kept the ring, though she had never worn it again after that last Christmas Ball in Calcutta. But probably because it had been James's mother's, Charlotte's grandmother. Once Grace learned about the ring, though, she couldn't pass it on to Charlotte. She would ask too many questions about it, and the answers would lead from one secret to another about her dysfunctional family. Grace definitely didn't want her daughter to be hurt discovering those secrets.

"Why are you doing this? I know you haven't worn it for years, but you can keep it." After a short pause, James added, "Please …"

Grace was shivering, but her voice was firm. "You know, life will always bring you back to the point where you went wrong. We all pay for our mistakes."

"It wasn't a mistake … our marriage wasn't a mistake!"

Grace turned to him. At that moment James looked so pitiful with his mouth open, trying to catch a dose of air, that her anger evaporated. As the last presence of whiskey disappeared somewhere in her bloodstream, she couldn't even bring herself to tell him about Thomas, his father. It would definitely hurt him more and who knew how he would handle it. She didn't want to be responsible for that.

"And your father … he didn't deserve that. Lord Clifford was a good man and you had a good life. What happened that night will haunt you forever."

She slowly started to walk out of the room.

"Grace, please. Grace …"

She stopped for a second, standing with her back towards James.

"Grace … I didn't want that to happen. He was my father! I just wanted … him to … love me back. I didn't want his or your pity. And … I loved you. I *still* love you … Grace."

She could hear he was crying. Did he say he *loved* her? And he admitted he loved his father. She told herself that she was right not to tell him about Thomas. It wouldn't help him or her. The room was stuffed with pain and suffering. Their lives were full of hurtful discoveries about each other. James wasn't in a good state, probably on the cusp of dying. Grace couldn't even look at him because she would feel sorry for him and then regret it. It was too late to fix anything between them. She didn't want to hear his confession. After all, he showed no sign of repentance. Even if his last words were full of anguish, he couldn't fetch the bullet back that he had fired at her and at their marriage a long time ago.

Wasting no more time, she said, "Goodbye … James." And she left.

After that, Grace and Charlotte had a long conversation at home. Charlotte didn't know about Grace's relationship with Aadir. When Grace told her that she would need to go to India and invited Charlotte to go with her, the questions started. So, Grace had to explain the reason for the trip. She told Charlotte as much as she could about her life in India before their journey. She shared her personal feelings with her daughter. Grace still loved Aadir and wanted to find him. She needed to tell him about their son and to ask Aadir to help her find his grave.

"Mum, of course, I will go with you. I had no idea what you went through and how much you suffered. I admire your strength and hunger for life. You have given me everything I needed. You are the most loving and caring mother. I love you, Mum." Grace received the most tender cuddle from her daughter.

Then, suddenly, Charlotte moved away from Grace and looked straight into her eyes.

"Mum, are you *sure* your son died?"

That was the question Grace had asked herself many times,

especially after reading Lord Clifford's letter. What if her son had survived? Hope flared inside her.

"I don't know, sweetheart. James showed me his death certificate, but, honestly, I don't know. Only Zia can reveal the truth. Only she knows what really happened that night and it's why I have to go to India. I need to find her and Aadir. I need to find the truth. And my son!" She paused for a second. "Dead or alive."

Part IV

India 1969

Calcutta

The Grand Hotel

Through the taxi window Grace watched the lively Calcutta streets while the car took them to the hotel. Charlotte was glued to the opposite window of the car as well, observing the scenes outside. *Although so much of this city has changed, a lot is still the same*, thought Grace. She saw people walking in their bare feet and observed the dust in the air created by cars and motorcycles. Women in saris tried to keep their balance holding heavy bundles on their heads while walking. The street noise and the busy market full of people selling food and clothes all overwhelmed her. A kaleidoscope of colour dazzled her eyes. Even through closed windows the smell of spices and cooked meat reached her nose. What hadn't changed were the people who always had smiles on their faces, on good days or bad. She waved back whenever she saw somebody looking at her. Children ran alongside the car. A warm rush of pleasant emotions swept over her and woke up her memories. It felt like she was coming back home.

A grandiose hotel appeared in front of them, and the taxi stopped.

"Mum, you didn't tell me that the hotel would be so beautiful. I'm impressed."

"I didn't know myself. Back then it looked a little bit different."

Both doors of the taxi opened at the same time. After getting out of the car, Grace and Charlotte found themselves standing on a carpet at the start of a long, wide staircase leading up to the front of the Grand Hotel. Grace and her daughter took in the building's ornate sign, the huge columns propping up the terrace with large elephant statues on both sides, and the wide steps covered with a beautiful red carpet on which there were patterns of flowers in gold. Despite the fact that many feet, of both staff and tourists, walked across it frequently, the carpet was clean and looked like new. Then they turned to admire the lawn in front of the hotel with its many marigolds. The sun shone brightly. Grace and Charlotte walked up the stairs to the front door, which was held open for them by the doormen stationed on both sides. They confidently entered the hotel.

In some parts, the interior was the same as in the 1940s, but Grace noticed that the drapes and wallpapers had changed. The furniture too. The corner of her eye caught two hardwood side tables, inlaid with an elephant pattern which she remembered from her last time there. These small mementos were touching. Grace placed a hand to her chest, admiring the interior of the huge entrance hall. The hotel staff smiled their welcome as they passed. Grace and Charlotte were shown to some sofas where they could rest while waiting for their room. In seconds, fresh lemonade and a few sweets were placed on the coffee table next to them. Charlotte couldn't believe how good the hotel service was.

Grace wasn't even sure if Aadir still lived in Calcutta. She knew nothing about him at all. For some reason she was afraid to see him again after so many years. When they had passed a mirror on the way in, she had stopped and looked at herself. Would Aadir recognise her? There were so many wrinkles on her face. There was none of the spark in her eyes that had been there at their first meeting. She definitely needed to freshen herself up.

The atmosphere in the hotel was relaxing with light, soft music playing in the background – just what they needed after their long journey. Charlotte asked Grace if she was feeling comfortable before she left to find the ladies' room. Grace sipped her cold lemonade and looked through the window at life beyond the hotel. Then she stood up and took a few steps before noticing a painting on the wall in a golden frame. She stared with wide eyes. It was one of her paintings that she had sold at the auction during her last Christmas Ball. She remembered that Aadir told her he had bought two of them; one was the golden orange sunset painting on the wall in front of her. Then she overheard Charlotte and turned towards the sound of her voice. Charlotte was talking to a young man, who was standing with his back to Grace. His uniform was different. He was probably the manager of the hotel.

Charlotte saw Grace and pointed at her and the young man turned around. Grace froze. Then she screamed, placing her hand over her mouth. Feeling dizzy, she raised her other hand to call for Charlotte; she couldn't utter a word. The man standing next to Charlotte was the double of Aadir. *This is not possible. I'm dreaming*, she thought before passing out.

The return of Angel

Back in time

On coming to, the first person Grace set eyes on was another young man in his late twenties, wearing a hotel staff uniform. She was lying on the sofa in the lounge and he was kneeling, staring at her in shock like she was a ghost. His face was familiar. Smiling now, he pointed with his finger first at her, then at himself and then at his wrist, on which hung a bracelet of multicoloured threads. Grace couldn't believe it. In front of her was the same boy who had hidden in her garden when she lived in India. She had made that bracelet for him. Was he real?

"Angel, is it you?" She touched his face. "I'm so happy to see you. I can't believe it. I thought … I didn't know what had happened to you. You disappeared. I waited and waited for you. Gosh, so many years passed. What are you doing here? How?"

As best as he could, using his hands and miming, Angel explained that he worked in the hotel, pointing to his hotel badge with the name *Angel*. Grace smiled and her eyes filled up with tears. Angel gave her a glass of water. She thanked him and took a couple of sips. He looked at Grace and shed tears as well. She moved her hand to show him that he should help her to rise from the sofa, and then she hugged him.

"So many years have passed," she said. "But it feels like yesterday since I saw you. How you have grown, my little Angel. Look at you."

Seeing Angel here, next to her, Grace suddenly felt much closer to Aadir. The scent of the incense in the hotel changed. There was something in the air that was impossible to catch, only those who had been close to each other twenty-two years ago could sense it.

Then she noticed Charlotte and a doctor next to her.

"Mum, you scared us all. We had to call a doctor. How are you feeling now. What was it?"

"Probably I'm just tired. Maybe I felt dizzy because of the smell of incense in the hotel. I'm fine now. Thanks, sweetheart. Who was that young man you were talking to?"

"Ah, that was Rakesh. He is the hotel manager's assistant. He was very kindly giving me directions. He saw me walking back from the ladies as I was lost in the hotel's many corridors."

At that moment Angel came back with the room keys and showed them the way to their suite. The doctor followed them. He wanted to make sure that Grace was well.

Reunited

True love never ends

After the doctor was satisfied that Grace was feeling better, he left. Charlotte couldn't hold her emotions in and ran around the tworoom suite like she was a child. Grace also acknowledged that the rooms were beautiful, spacious and bright with a few nice pieces of furniture, just how she liked it. A tray with tea was brought to the room straight away. After they finished, Charlotte went downstairs to the reception as she had forgotten her scarf there. When the door closed behind Charlotte, Grace closed her eyes and tried to relax, comfortably resting on the sofa. But about five minutes later a knock on the door got her attention.

"Charlotte, is that you? The door is open."

To her astonishment, she saw that it was Aadir standing at the door. A new tide of emotion flooded in; Grace's chest was heaving for air.

Aadir rushed to her. "Grace! My love."

He got on his knees in front of her and took her hands in his. The warmth of his hands brought her to her senses. He kissed every finger, bowing his head, with his eyes closed. Then he looked up to Grace. Her wideopen eyes drowned in his, which were full of love. She could see it. Aadir had the same love for her in his gaze as he had before. She couldn't believe he was next to her. Grace slowly lifted her hand up and touched Aadir's ebony, wavy hair, which was already greying, but still soft. He was as handsome as he had been twenty-two years ago. Electricity flowed between them, like the first time they met; the same lightning shot through and connected them when they touched. Then they were kissing, almost suffocating each other, while Aadir tenderly held Grace's head, caressing her hair. Out of breath, they stopped kissing and their eyes met. They were silent for a moment. There were not enough words to say what they wanted to say but both were just happy to be reunited. It was a while before they moved. Then Aadir sat next to Grace on the sofa, holding her in his arms. She rested her head on his shoulder.

"Aadir ..."

"Yes, my love?" He immediately looked at her.

"I can't believe that I'm seeing you."

"Me neither, my love."

"How did you find out I was here?"

"I received a phone call about a beautiful English lady who fainted in the foyer of my hotel."

"Your hotel?"

"Yes, my love. The hotel where we met and fell in love. It's a long story. I will tell you later. How are you feeling now? You scared us all."

"I am good, thanks. I am better, but … confused."

"Oh, Grace, I'm soo happy to see you!" Aadir embraced her tightly.

"And how happy I am too! Aadir, I think I'm dreaming. I came to India to find you and you found me. And where? In the Grand Hotel, your hotel!"

"Yes, like twenty-two years ago I found you here. This hotel has memories for both of us. I treasure them every day. Do you know I always keep the 'Reserved' sign on the table we sat at for tea?"

"Do you? Ah, Aadir, I would love to have tea at that table again."

"And you will, my love! Why did *you* choose this hotel?"

"The Grand is the only hotel I know. And for the same reason: I met you here." Grace tried to smile but felt nervous. "Aadir, I saw … Angel. I was happy to see him and know that the boy is fine."

"Yes, he works in the hotel now. It took me a couple of years before I found him, back at the beginning of the 1950s. He was ill for a long time, and one family took him in. Then I saw him wandering around the house where you lived. He was looking for you. I explained to him that you left. He cried. I took him with me."

"Thank you so much for looking after him. He is a lovely boy and very smart too."

"He is, you are right. He missed you a lot. We all missed you, Grace."

"Aadir, I also saw …" Grace didn't know where to start. They could talk about other things for hours, but they both knew, they had to discuss the events that had separated them.

"Rakesh. You already saw Rakesh?" His calming voice helped her.

"Is that the same Rakesh who was talking to Charlotte?"

"It was Rakesh, my love."

"Aadir, I'm …"

"You better know everything, Grace. We have both waited for so long. *You* waited for so long, my love. I want you to know that I did search for you."

"You did?"

"Yes. I searched back then in 1947 and for many years after. Please understand that when James took you away, the chaos started. Not just on the plantations, but everywhere in the country. Political unrest, tensions rising from all sides. Our nation cried out for independence."

"I heard about it, Aadir, but I had just lost my child and was brought back to England in a semi-conscious state. I don't remember much of it. You know I loved and still love India. I'm really happy your country is now independent. All I'm asking is, why didn't you look harder for me?"

"I know, I don't have any justification for that. Forgive me please, my love. I learned from Zia that you were in Kurseong for a few months where ..." He closed his eyes for a second taking a deep breath. "You gave birth to your son. I'm so sorry, my love, I wasn't there with you. I'm so sorry. It wouldn't have made any difference for me who the father of your child was. Please believe me, I would still have wanted to be with you." Aadir kissed Grace on her cheeks, eyes and forehead. His eyes quickly filled up with tears.

Grace held back her own tears. She couldn't determine what she felt at that moment. She was sad that he hadn't looked for her hard enough and hadn't told her everything earlier.

"We tried to send a message to you. Zia did everything possible to contact you in Darjeeling."

"I didn't know about it at that time, my love. We left Darjeeling soon after you. James came back two days after he took you away because Oliver was leaving, and they met to finalise things about the last tea exportation. Your husband came around to our house and threatened me. So, we decided it would be better for us to leave. It was clear he was furious and might do something that would hurt you."

"He threatened you? I didn't even know he went back to the plantations. He never mentioned that."

"I discovered later that James had been talking to the

plantation workers before you left. It must have been one of the workers who told him something. Maybe somebody saw me that morning …"

"But he didn't say anything to me. He just …" Grace stopped, thinking fast and decided in the end not to tell Aadir about the last night on the plantations and what James *did* to her. Her wound was healed, but it might hurt Aadir.

"He played his game. He said if I ever tried to contact you, he would …"

"He would do what?"

Aadir repeated James's words to Grace. "'If you ever try to contact my wife, she will suffer and that will be *your* fault. I could accuse you and my wife of adultery and you know the implications of that for both of you.'"

Grace looked away and said, "He made me suffer anyway."

Aadir immediately opened his arms and hugged her. Grace couldn't hold her tears in anymore. She cried. He hugged her even tighter.

Aadir was still holding Grace in his arms when he said, "I see the scars on your heart in your eyes, my love. You've suffered enough. He truly is a monster. You know, when Zia came back, she was shivering for months, poor girl."

"So, it was Zia?"

"Yes, Zia saved your child. She saved *our* son."

"*Our* son. So, you knew?"

The word *son* was so precious for Grace. She said it and dropped her head on Aadir's shoulder. He held her gently and kissed her hair. She could hear his heart pumping as fast as hers. Then she pushed him away and started to punch him in his chest with her fists.

"Why didn't you tell me earlier. Why?"

"Grace, my love, I couldn't."

"Why couldn't you? I thought my son died. I thought my son was *his* son. I wanted to die. How could you do this to me? You? Twenty-two years!"

He accepted her blows without resistance. "I tried, my love. I did."

"You tried what? When?" She stopped punching him.

"When Rakesh was about five years old, I went to England."

"You went to England? I cannot believe it! And?"

"I did. My father helped me to find the address of Lord Clifford in London, but his neighbour told me that you lived at a different address. I finally found your house. I saw you in the garden with a little girl in your arms. James was next to you. You looked happy. I thought you had moved on and stayed with James, that you had a daughter. I didn't know what to do. There were the three of you, together. I could not stop staring at you. I remember your smile and the smile of your daughter. I couldn't take that away from you and he wouldn't have allowed that to happen. So, I left. My heart was broken.

But I never stopped loving you, Grace. Never!"

"That was Charlotte, Aadir. She is Molly and Oliver's daughter. They died in a car accident. She's my adopted daughter. You were so close to me and I didn't know. Do you know how much that hurts? You could have left a message, Aadir, or somehow let me know that you were in London." Grace tilted her head up to the ceiling, keeping her tears from falling.

"My love. I couldn't take the risk. Do you know what James said to Zia? He also threatened her. He said that if Zia or I ever searched for you and told you about your son, he would kill you."

"Kill me?" She shuddered.

"My father begged me not to go to England. He was scared of something happening to you, to me or to Rakesh, whom James called … a halfcaste bastard."

"He called our son a what?!" Grace's eyes were the size of the moon. She was livid.

"You are better not hearing everything he said that night to Zia. All these years we lived worrying that he might do something to you. We worried for *you*, Grace. Because after he took you away, the next day, when I drove my car to town, the brakes didn't work. Thankfully I found out in time. Then there was a fire in our house on the plantations. Some of the workers believed that James was involved in all of this. It wasn't safe for us to stay there. But I never stopped believing I would see you again. We just needed time. I accepted the direction our lives took. I had to get married."

"That was the last news I received about you, your marriage. Soon after I gave birth to our son."

"Zia told me everything. I had to get married, my love. That's our tradition. Yes, my father maybe rushed with the wedding. He just wanted James to stop threatening us. And then a few months later my wife kindly accepted Rakesh. I was grateful to her. She died five years later from typhoid. It was then I came to England to find you."

"So sorry to hear about your wife. I am not angry, Aadir, not anymore. Thanks to you both for raising Rakesh. I can't wait to see him. Where is he? Does he know about me?"

"He knows now. My father was very ill recently. He didn't want to die with all the secrets in our family still hidden, so we told Rakesh about his grandmother, Helen, and about you. Rakesh was very angry with me. I told him that we would go to England together to find you. I just needed to sort out a few things in the hotel. It's hard for me, but I understand him. I went through this myself, not knowing about my real mother. I am giving him time and space to digest all that information. I kept one photo of you from the 1940s and gave it to Rakesh. He wanted to know everything about you. Just last month he asked me about where you lived in India, and then he went to see the place."

"Oh, Aadir. What are we going to do? I hope he won't be angry with me. I didn't even see him after he was born. What can I say to him? Will he understand and accept me? I couldn't do anything. They took him away from me."

Grace felt the weight of guilt bearing down on her, but Aadir helped her by saying, "That was your cruel and sinister husband. Grace, I can't even imagine what you went through. My love, I wish I had been there for you." He took both of her hands in his and lifted them up to his lips, kissing them. "Don't worry, Rakesh won't be angry with you. That wasn't your fault. He knows that. He might be angry with me, but he was keen to see you. He wanted to go to England without me. I stopped him and it made him even more angry. I just needed time to prepare him properly to meet you."

"Can we be prepared for that, Aadir? I was told my son was dead. That *evil man* showed me his death certificate."

"How did he get that? We actually tried to find the doctor to recover Rakesh's birth certificate. I went to Kurseong, but there was no sign of the doctor and no baby was registered on that day. He probably bribed the doctor to make a false death certificate."

"He is capable of many things, but I didn't know he could do such a terrible thing as faking my son's death."

"Grace, how did you find out?"

"My father-in-law, Lord Clifford. He wrote a letter for me

before he died in 1948, but, unfortunately, I only received that letter a month ago. He said in it that James couldn't have children. Can you believe it? And James had been telling me all these years that he lost *his* son too. He pretended he was grieving … It makes me sick thinking of the time I lived under the same roof as him. But I had to, for Charlotte."

"What kind of man is he? So, he knew from the beginning that he wasn't the father of your child and … made such an evil plan to get rid of your baby. I can't … If I ever see him I will … with my own hands!"

"You don't need to. The fire did that for you."

"Fire?"

"Yes, he went to see his father and somehow managed to start a fire in the house. He, of course, was drunk. Unfortunately, Lord Clifford couldn't be saved. James lost an eye and half of his body was burned beyond recognition. He hasn't been able to walk since then."

"Half of his body? Lucky devil."

Grace looked pensively at the floor and began saying, "There was something else in that letter …" when the door opened.

Rakesh

The family

Cheerful, Charlotte came into the room with a big bouquet of fresh red roses in her hands. She was so excited that she didn't immediately notice her mother and Aadir. Charlotte turned back and, gesturing with her eyes, invited a young man to follow her into their suite.

"Mum, look what Rakesh gave us as a complimentary gift from the hotel."

At that moment silence enveloped the room. Charlotte stopped at the door holding the flowers and looked with surprise at her mother in Aadir's arms. Grace glanced at Rakesh standing behind Charlotte. Aadir's eyes moved from Charlotte to his son. Rakesh observed everybody in the room. Aadir stood up first, in silence, and helped Grace to get up from the sofa. Charlotte slowly walked towards the table near the door to put the flowers down and stood there speechless. A strange feeling filled the room. Grace and Rakesh stared at each other.

Grace had lived so many years in anger and frustration

because of the loss of her son. She had been very ill and had survived depression. She had wanted to die. The haunting nightmare had exhausted her. Her husband's manipulative tricks, demands and blackmail had distracted her from searching for the truth and from even thinking about going back to India.

And Aadir had kept their son's survival a secret for twenty-two years! She didn't know that he had been raised by his father; she had been left bereft of the joy of experiencing motherhood and seeing him grow up. And yet, after all that, which surely gave her every right to be angry with both James and Aadir, she found that she couldn't be.

At that moment, when Grace saw her son, she could feel only overwhelming bliss at seeing him *alive*. Her son was alive! She quickly decided she wouldn't dwell on how he had survived. He had survived! Her eyes, full of tears, were smiling. It was a moment of magic. It overcame all anger and unlocked her heart, releasing the eternal love she had carefully kept inside for her son. It wasn't an illusion. She felt like the nightmare had finally been driven from her mind, her body and from her life. She was overjoyed.

"Rakesh …" she whispered softly.

Her legs were getting wobbly, her heart beating fast. Yet, she managed to see his face in detail. His hair, the shape of his eyes, the line of his lips. There was no more evidence needed to understand that before her stood *her* son. A mother's heart could tell the truth. She had been twenty-five years old when she gave birth to him. She was forty-seven years old now.

Aadir made a move towards Rakesh.

"Rakesh, we have to tell you …"

Rakesh stopped his father from speaking, raising his hand, and slowly started to walk towards Grace. He passed his father without even looking at him. When he came close to Grace, she held out her hands in front of her and Rakesh immediately took them in his. She could feel their warmth. *He is such a lovely boy*, she thought. *My boy. My son. So handsome and grown up.*

"My baby … my dear son." Grace exhaled loudly and opened her arms wide.

"Mother …" Rakesh didn't wait for any longer. He clung to her. The love which Grace had kept in her heart for so many years was poured into their warm and loving embrace. They connected instantly, as mother and son.

The heavy burden of time was lifted from all three of them. The room seemed to grow brighter. Tears flowed as they all smiled and cried at the same time. No one could utter a word. Were words needed? They had been waiting for this moment for so long, they were afraid to lose it. A miracle had happened. Grace couldn't believe that her son was in her arms. She moved her hands over his back, making sure he was real.

"Rakesh, my dearest. Deep in my heart I knew you were alive. Forgive me, forgive me please. I should have trusted my feelings and come back to India sooner … and found you."

"Mother … I didn't know about you … I would have come to you myself."

When Rakesh called her "Mother", Grace's heart melted. Her son's voice was the sweetest sound in the world to her.

"My son, Rakesh. There are events which happened in the past that if we could have done more about or changed at the time, we would have. But we couldn't. Nobody could. Fate had other plans for us. Your father and I hope you can forgive us."

He looked at her with admiration. "I'm not angry with you, Mother. I am so happy to see you!"

"Thank you, Rakesh. Me too, very happy!" Grace hugged him. "Please, don't be angry with your father either. He raised you and looked after you. And look what a handsome young man you are!" She ruffled the hair on his forehead. They smiled softly at each other.

"Mum?" Everybody turned to Charlotte.

"Charlotte. Oh, sorry, my darling. Rakesh, this is my daughter Charlotte and …" she paused "Charlotte, please meet my son, Rakesh. So sorry. I was wrapped up in my emotions."

"We have met already." Charlotte held out her hand to him. "But, nice to meet you again, Rakesh."

Rakesh held Charlotte's hand in both of his for a few seconds, looking at her eyes curiously. "Nice to meet you too, Charlotte."

Then Aadir and Charlotte shook hands.

"What a surprise for all of us. Who would have expected we would find you both so quickly. What a day! I guess, we need champagne!"

Grace glanced over at Aadir. "Why not?" And she sat back on the sofa.

Rakesh sat down next to his mother. Aadir invited Charlotte to go with him to choose the best champagne. Then he suggested that he also get the best table in the restaurant ready for dinner that night to celebrate their reunion, before leaving the room with Charlotte, giving Grace space to be with her son.

But just before dinner, Grace received an unexpected telegram.

Knot on a thread

Nobody owns the truth

Grace stood on the terrace looking up to the sky. She was in the same hotel and the same spot where she had been standing almost twenty-four years ago, when she met Aadir. It was a warm evening as usual. She was overwhelmed with happy feelings and emotions after the family dinner at the hotel. The only thing she wanted to forget was that call from reception, just before they had all gathered around the table. It was a telegram from her lawyer in London. He had sent it to inform her about the death of her husband, James.

She recalled standing there for a moment with the telegram in her hands reading the note at the end that said James's last words were … calling for his mother. She held her breath for a second and then exhaled, wishing James rest in peace, then quickly tore it up and threw it in the bin next to the reception. Before she could process the information, Aadir came over.

"Is everything all right, my love? Was that something important?"

Grace paused for a second. "Not important. I will tell you later. Let's go back and have a great time with our children."

Aadir agreed with her and, offering his arm, he slowly and graciously walked her through the big hall, along the long corridor and then up the wide stairs covered with a timeless oriental carpet, to the restaurant upstairs. Grace was engrossed in her conversation with him.

"I will be grateful to Thomas for the rest of my life for this hotel."

"How so? Did he help you buy it?"

"More than that! It was his gift to me. He told me before he died that, when his business partner left India in 1948, he bought his partner's shares, and then he left the Grand Hotel to me in his Will. I was very grateful to him for what he had already done for me and didn't expect this."

"It seems Thomas was a decent and very generous man. What about your father?"

"My father, with all the money he saved from the work for Lord Clifford, was only able to open a small tea shop in Calcutta after he left the tea plantations. There were hard times, but we survived."

"I am sorry, Aadir, for what happened to your father. He shouldn't have lost his job."

"He wouldn't have had that job if not for Lord Clifford. My father hated James, but he appreciated that he was able to provide for his family because of that job. Before he died, he said that there was some kind of secret between him and Lord

Clifford that kept him earning money. I was shocked to learn about it."

"Secret? Did he tell you what that secret was?"

"No. He was very weak in his last days and I didn't want to ask him again about it. And I didn't think it was that important for me to know, if my father could keep it for all his life without telling me."

"Did it ever bother you, what it could be?"

"No, my love, never. It wasn't my secret and I had no desire to discover it. If it was something involving me, it will find me sooner or later. Or it may never come to me. Why should I search for something I don't need to know about? I have everything I need. *We* have everything we need, my love."

"I have to thank Thomas too. By the way, what was his second name?"

"Howard. Thomas Howard. Why?"

Goosebumps covered Grace's skin. She pulled her silky scarf back over her shoulders. "Just curious. Did you tell Rakesh about him?"

"I did. I had to. When I told him about you, he asked me if there were more secrets. I told Rakesh how I found out about my mother and about Thomas. So, he could see he wasn't the only one who was kept in the dark for years and that there was always a reason for that. Sometimes secrets are there to be revealed at the right time and place. We learn that through our life experiences, don't we, Grace?"

With that they walked into the restaurant. Rakesh and Charlotte were immersed in a conversation like they had known each other for years. It was a sweet moment for Grace to see. By the smile on Aadir's face, she understood it was the same for him too. They even stopped for a moment, watching their children talking and laughing. That dinner was the best time of Grace's life. It was the first time she felt her life was complete; she was a mother and a woman who was loved by a man she loved. She had a family now, peace and could see a future for herself.

It had been an enjoyable evening, but Grace couldn't sleep that night. She couldn't help wondering what the right thing was to do now. On the one hand she had been left with a secret about Thomas. On the other, was it her place to tell that secret and what purpose would it serve?

Grace thought about Aadir, who had learned about his mother later in his life, not from his father, but from Thomas. And about Lord Clifford who hadn't told his son James that he wasn't his father and who had died with that secret, leaving Grace to decide what to do with it. And James, for whom even the one secret he carried in his life was too much. He had never recovered from the grief of his mother's death and finding out that he couldn't have children must have been a terrible blow. He had never found the courage to tell her about it after they got married and the consequences were high, for both of them, but most hurtful for Grace.

Thinking of all these past secrets, she found herself now in the same position. A feeling of guilt twisted her stomach. She now knew that Thomas, who was James's father, was the man who had looked after Aadir and had left him everything after he died. Thomas and James died not knowing about each other. Would that secret help her and Aadir after it was revealed? And if she did not reveal it, would she be the same as all of them, the ones who kept their secrets? How would Rakesh and Charlotte take it? She didn't want to hurt anyone. She was trying hard to find a solution, which was why she had decided to come and stand on the terrace that night. She was searching for an answer. Was it her secret to tell?

"I knew I would find you here."

Aadir covered her shoulders with a silk shawl. Then he walked around to stand next to her. Putting his arm behind her back, he gently pulled her towards him.

"Grace, I love you so much! More and more with every day. I can only breathe and sleep because of you. I will never let you leave my side again, never!"

"I love you very much too, Aadir." She placed her head on his shoulder and leaned closer to him. She felt loved and at peace in Aadir's most tender embrace.

"This time no one can stand between us and no more secrets."

"No... more... secrets ..." replied Grace, drawing out each word.

Epilogue

Donegal, Ireland

Curling waves impatiently caressed the Atlantic Ocean, loudly breaking and scattering in white foam along the sandy beach. The sun was hiding behind the clouds, but the wind mercifully brought a warm breeze to the Donegal shore, after three days of rain. It was a perfect May day for a long walk on the beach. But Grace took her time. She sat on the wooden bench next to the blossomed hawthorn tree. The one she was born under. The rich smell of wet earth and nourished green grass pleased her. She touched the plaque on the bench, put there in memory of her mother.

Nora O'Donnell-Bellmore 1898–1924

She softly said, "Sorry, Mum, for taking so long to come back."

Her gaze slowly moved towards the horizon where a line of light from the sun's rays breaking through the clouds divided the ocean and sky. The cries of seagulls sounded like they were calling for her. Grace started walking. She took off her shoes when she reached the grassy dunes; the pleasant sensation of touching warm sand instantly passed from her feet up through her body. A grateful smile formed on her lips and her eyes lit up. The playful wind gently loosened a few strands of her hair. She was in good spirits and felt blessed. With every step towards the ocean, Grace felt happy and complete.

“Nobody owns the truth.
Truth owns everybody”

Tatiana Tierney